"I make you a small proposition,"

Jean-Claude said. "For the pleasure of your company in my suite, I will pay you back all the money you have lost, and five hundred dollars more."

Sam stood stock-still for a moment. She wasn't sure she had heard him correctly. "Are you telling me that you'll pay me fourteen hundred dollars *if I'll go to your suite with you?"*

"This is correct," Jean-Claude said. "Your problems would be solved, no? It is so simple."

"Not so simple," Sam answered, brushing some hair out of her face. "What am I supposed to be doing in your suite to earn all this money?"

"Samantha, you are too young to be so cynical," Jean-Claude chided her.

"Oh, re ... ere I come fro ... only one thing- ... k you mean."

The SUNSET ISLAND series
by Cherie Bennett

Sunset Island
Sunset Kiss
Sunset Dreams
Sunset Farewell
Sunset Reunion
Sunset Secrets
Sunset Heat
Sunset Promises
Sunset Scandal
Sunset Whispers
Sunset Paradise

Sunset Paradise

Cherie Bennett

SPLASH™

A BERKLEY / SPLASH BOOK

SUNSET PARADISE is an original publication
of The Berkley Publishing Corporation.
This work has never appeared before in book form.

SUNSET PARADISE

A Berkley Book / published by arrangement with
General Licensing Company, Inc.

PRINTING HISTORY
Berkley edition / December 1992

A GLC BOOK

Splash is a trademark belonging to
General Licensing Company, Inc.

ISBN: 0-425-13770-8

A BERKLEY BOOK ® TM 757,375
Berkley Books are published by The Berkley Publishing Group,
200 Madison Avenue, New York, New York 10016.
The name "BERKLEY" and the "B" logo
are trademarks belonging to Berkley Publishing Corporation.

PRINTED IN THE UNITED STATES OF AMERICA

10 9 8 7 6 5 4 3 2 1

**For the man with the
honey-bear eyes**

ONE

"This rain is mondo depressing," Sam sighed as she stared out the sliding glass doors that led to the Hewitts' deck. The rain was pelting the doors so hard that the backyard was just a blur of greenery.

"This was the only day Kurt actually had a couple of hours to spend at the beach with me," Emma said glumly.

"It's rained every day for a week," Carrie added, as if they didn't all know that already.

The three best friends, Samantha Bridges, Carrie Alden, and Emma Cresswell, sighed simultaneously as the storm seemed to gather force outside.

"I'm starting to take this personally," Sam grumbled. "This may be nature's way of telling us we're having too much fun."

Well, they *were* having fun—that was

something all three of them could agree about.

As Sam stared out at the rain she thought about all the exciting—as well as complicated—things that were going on in her life.

She had a great summer job as an au pair on ritzy Sunset Island, where she lived with Dan Jacobs and his twin fourteen-year-old daughters, Allie and Becky. She spent a lot of time hanging out with her two best friends, who were also au pairs. She was dating a totally buff guy named Pres Travis, who was the bass player with the hot rock band Flirting with Danger—or the Flirts, as they were commonly known. On top of that, she'd recently auditioned to be a backup singer/dancer for the Flirts, and she'd been hired, as had Emma!

Then there was the complicated stuff. Although she was incredibly attracted to Pres, she couldn't seem to stop flirting with other guys. But it made her crazy when other girls flirted with Pres, especially if he seemed to be flirting back. The whole thing gave her a huge headache—she wasn't sure *what* she really wanted.

And then there was the really big confusion. She'd found out earlier in the summer that she was adopted—*adopted!*—and that for nineteen years her parents had neglected to mention it. Through Family Finders, a nonprofit organization that helps people find their birth parents, she'd recently met her birth mother.

Susan Briarly—Sam couldn't think of her as "Mother," since she already had one of those—had come to the island to meet Sam, and since then they'd been corresponding. Now Sam's feelings were a mass of confusion—about her adoptive parents, who had lied to her, about Susan, who had given her up at birth, even about Susan's kids, who had only just been told that she existed.

"I have to have my pink Mickey Mouse sneakers!" Sam heard a little girl's voice insist from the next room. "Mickey wants to see them!"

Sam knew it had to be four-year-old Katie Hewitt, one of the three kids who were in Emma's charge.

"Hey, Em, you haven't by any chance seen Katie's pink sneakers, have you?" Jeff Hewitt asked, sticking his head into the kitchen. "Katie is convinced that she has to wear them to Disney World, or Mickey will throw her out."

The Hewitt family was leaving the next morning for a week-long trip to visit Jane's mother in Miami Beach, Florida. Then Jane and Jeff were planning to rent a car and drive the kids to Orlando to see Disney

World. Lucky Emma would have more than a whole week off to do whatever she wanted.

"I'll help you look," Emma offered, getting up from the kitchen table.

"There's a picture of Mickey on them," Katie said helpfully, coming into the kitchen behind her father.

"I know that, cutie," Emma said, playfully tickling Katie in the ribs. "Come on, let's go look under the furniture in the family room." Emma took Katie's hand and they walked away.

"She's so good with kids," Sam commented to Carrie. "You'd never know she was a filthy-rich heiress and an only child."

"Do I hear jealousy rearing its ugly little green head?" Carrie teased Sam.

Sam shook her red curls back from her face. "*Moi?*" she asked innocently. "Jealous of Emma, just because she's actually lived the lifestyle of the rich and famous, whereas I have only dreamed about it? Perish the thought!"

Carrie drained the last of the Diet Coke from her glass. "Listen, I have no doubt that those dreams of yours will become reality one day."

"You think?" Sam asked, pleased at her friend's vote of confidence.

"I don't think, I know," Carrie said. "I

mean, look at you. You're gorgeous, smart, and talented. What's to stop you?"

"Yeah, what?" Sam agreed. She stood up and walked over to the sliding glass doors, where she watched the rain beating down for a moment. Then she turned back to Carrie. "Sometimes I wonder, though."

"What?" Carrie asked.

"Well, Emma is in college, and you go to Yale, for pete's sake. . . ." Sam's voice trailed off.

"You had a dance scholarship to Kansas State," Carrie reminded Sam. "You were the one who dropped out after only a few weeks of school so you could dance professionally at Disney World."

"I *know* that," Sam said testily, irritated that Carrie was reminding her. Sam was also the one who had gotten fired from Disney World for being too original, and she didn't want to be reminded of *that*, either. "It's just that sometimes I wonder if an education might not be a good thing."

"Well, of course it's a good thing!" Carrie exclaimed. "Hey, are you thinking about going back to college in the fall?"

"No," Sam said. "Forget I said anything."

"But—" Carrie began.

"Once again I have saved the day!" Emma called out, walking back into the kitchen.

She was soaking wet, but she looked happy. "I remembered how much Dog loves Katie's shoes," she said, referring to the family pet—named by Katie. She opened the closet for a towel and started to dry herself off. "He had them socked away in his doghouse in the backyard."

"Good thing," Sam said. "They *do* throw you out of Disney World if you're not wearing the official Mickey Mouse footgear," she said seriously.

"Was that your downfall?" Carrie asked, a smile on her face.

"I was simply too good for them," Sam said with dignity. *Right. As if it doesn't still smart that Mr. Christopher fired me*, she added to herself. So what if the choreographer had told her how talented she was? He'd still fired her, and it still made her feel like a failure.

"I gotta get back to work," Sam said, pushing all thoughts of Disney World from her mind. "I promised I'd take the monsters on a shopping spree this afternoon. I'm trying to be Little Miss Perfect so Mr. Jacobs won't get ticked about our having another gig with the Flirts tonight."

"Why, does he think you're spending too much time on the band?" Carrie asked, taking their glasses to the sink.

"He's actually really nice about it," Sam admitted. She picked up her purse and pulled out her car keys. "Of course, tonight the monsters are coming to the Play Café to watch us perform, so it's sort of like killing two birds with one stone."

"I have to get going, too," Carrie said. "So I'll see you guys at the café tonight. Are you two nervous that Graham and Claudia will be there?"

Carrie was the au pair of Graham and Claudia Templeton. Graham was better known as Graham Perry, rock superstar. The Flirts were friends of theirs, and that night Graham and Claudia were coming to hear the Flirts perform with their new backup singer/dancers.

"Who, a seasoned pro like me?" Emma asked with a laugh. Sam and Carrie knew that before auditioning for the Flirts, Emma hadn't sung in public since her days in a madrigal group at boarding school in Switzerland.

"There's a little pressure," Sam acknowledged. "I mean, the guys know just how much Graham could help us if he wanted to. Graham could even ask us to tour with him!"

"Which would mean good-bye au pair jobs," Emma pointed out.

Sam laughed. "Somehow I think that if I

get the chance to tour with Graham Perry, I'll get over my deep sadness at leaving the monsters behind." She waved at her friends. "I'm outta here!"

Sam's mind wandered as she drove back to the Jacobses' house. She really did feel good about her life, and she didn't particularly want to go back to college. And yet sometimes she wondered whether she was missing some essential experience and would end up sorry years from now. That was what her parents always said, and maybe they were right. . . . *Fat chance,* Sam told herself. She stopped at a light and peered out through the windshield at the pouring rain. *I'm more a make-things-happen-now kind of babe. My parents are totally wrong.*

"Becky! Allie!" Sam called when she ran into the house. She shook the droplets of water off herself and sorted through the mail sitting on the hall table. She saw Susan Briarly's familiar stationery, the envelope addressed to her in Susan's girlish, slanted handwriting. *This is the second time she's written me back before I've written to her,* Sam realized. *So sue me. I'm a terrible correspondent.* She pocketed the letter and went in search of the twins. She found them in the den, listening intently to some music through a dual set of headphones.

"Hi there," Sam said, pulling one headphone off Becky's ear. She knew it was Becky—Allie had cut her hair a while back, when she had wanted the world to see that she and her identical twin were two different people.

"Hey, I'm trying to concentrate here!" Becky snapped, and put the headphones back in place.

"Fine," Sam muttered, though she knew neither girl could hear her. She picked up the copy of *Rock On* magazine that was sitting on the coffee table and plopped down on the couch to read.

Some time later, after Sam had read an article about a new female rap group and an exposé on the secret life of Janet Jackson, the twins pulled off their headphones.

"I think Jim Morrison was God," Becky said solemnly.

"No lie," Allie agreed.

"You were listening to an old Doors tape?" Sam asked.

"Yeah, the greatest-hits one," Allie said. "Our band is going to cover some of their tunes."

"Done the Zit People way, of course," Becky added.

"Of course," Sam agreed seriously.

Lord Whitehead and the Zit People was the band Becky and Allie sang—or rather chanted—backup for. The leader of the band was thirteen-year-old Ian Templeton, Graham's son. Ian had invented something he called industrial music. He and his friends banged on household appliances while a tape of famous rock music played. Then they chanted rhythmically along with the chorus of the tune. Sam had heard them play, and as awful as the music sounded, the band was actually getting kind of good, in a bizarre sort of way.

"We're going to do 'Light My Fire,'" Becky said. "Ian says it can be a political statement about the apathy of youth in an overindustrialized society. We're going to set fire to a microwave while we all chant 'Light my fire, light my fire, light my fire.'"

"Uh-huh," Sam said, trying to keep a straight face. "Let's just hope that wherever you're performing has fire insurance."

"Oh, very amusing," Allie scoffed.

"We're totally on the cutting edge of music," Becky told Sam, "which is more than I can say for the Flirts."

Sam rolled her eyes. She'd told them they were too young to be backups for the Flirts, and so ever since they'd joined Ian's band, they'd been extremely competitive with her.

"We're not trying to be on the cutting edge," Sam said. "We're just trying to be good."

"Well, we'll give you our professional critique after we hear you tonight," Becky said loftily.

"Now there's something to look forward to," Sam said under her breath as she got off the couch. "You two want to eat something before we go shopping?" she asked them.

"We made a pizza," Allie informed her. "There's a piece left on the kitchen table, if you want it."

Sam walked into the kitchen, which looked as if a hurricane had hit it. There were shreds of mozzarella cheese on the counter and on the floor. Mushrooms, onions, and peppers had been left out on the counter. Some pepperoni had been ground into the floor under someone's heel. Two dirty dishes sat on the kitchen table, with, as promised, one lonely, congealed-looking slice of pizza left on a cookie sheet.

Sam swore softly and popped the slice of pizza in the microwave. Then she strode purposefully back into the den. "You left the kitchen a mess," she said in a level voice, fighting the urge to scream at them.

"Oh, yeah," Becky said laconically.

"We got involved in our music," Allie added.

"Well, now that you're uninvolved, would you please clean up?" Sam asked.

"You can do it," Becky said casually, looking through some tapes.

"I could, but I'm not going to," Sam told her. She stood there waiting patiently while the twins purposely ignored her.

Sam sighed heavily. Why did Becky and Allie have to make it so difficult? They could be such angels at times, but at other times they more than earned Sam's nickname for them—the monsters.

"Look, let me make myself clear," Sam said. "Either you two go clean up the kitchen or I'm not taking you shopping and you're not coming to the Play Café tonight to hear the Flirts."

That got their attention.

"Who are you supposed to be, our mother?" Allie asked.

"Yeah, since when do you get to make the rules?" Becky put in.

"I'm not the servant in this house, and I'm not cleaning up after you," Sam snapped. She turned on her heel and marched back into the kitchen just as the buzzer went off on the microwave. *Hey, that's the first time I ever gave the twins an ultimatum without checking with their father first,* Sam realized as she slid the pizza out of the microwave. For a moment she wondered if she'd overstepped her bounds. She might not be a servant, but she was, after all, an employee.

The next thing she knew, though, the twins were in the kitchen, silently cleaning up. *It worked!* Sam thought exultantly, nibbling at her slice of pizza. *It actually worked!* She was careful to keep her face expressionless, lest the twins know how triumphant she felt. Maybe Emma wasn't the only one who was good with kids!

Two hours later, Becky, Allie, and Sam pushed open the front door to the Cheap Boutique, the hippest place on the island to buy clothes. "Light My Fire" was blaring through the sound system.

"It's like some kind of sign!" Becky marveled before she and her sister ran to the back of the store, where the wilder clothes were displayed.

"Hey, Sam!" a friendly voice called.

Sam turned around to see Darcy Laken, a girl she'd met through Emma. Darcy was as tall as Sam, but had a fuller build. She looked athletic and strong, which is exactly what she was. She also had long black hair to die for, and startlingly lovely violet eyes.

Sam noted her white jeans and the violet tank top that emphasized her remarkable eye color.

"Hi, Darcy," Sam said happily, pleased to see her.

It was funny, really, because at first she hadn't liked Darcy very much at all. Darcy was very direct—outspoken, even—and it had taken Sam by surprise. *Maybe she just reminded me too much of myself*, Sam mused. Anyway, she'd come to see that Darcy was a genuine, loyal friend with a great sense of humor. On top of that, she was slightly psychic, which added an element of mystery and glamor to her that Sam simply couldn't resist.

"Is this one of those shop-till-you-drop days?" Darcy teased.

"For the twins, maybe," Sam said. "I'm supposed to be on something called a—yuck—budget."

"Tell me about it." Darcy laughed. "The last time I bought myself anything was for my high school graduation, and even then it was on sale!"

"So what are you springing for today?" Sam asked, pushing her curls behind one ear.

"Something for Molly," Darcy said. "Something terrific. I'll know it when I see it."

Darcy was referring to sixteen-year-old Molly Mason. Darcy lived at the Masons' hilltop mansion—some people said it was haunted—and took care of Molly, who was a paraplegic due to a terrible car accident only months earlier. She also knew that Molly, who before her accident had been quite independent and fearless, hated going out in public in her wheelchair.

"You couldn't get Molly to come?" Sam asked.

Darcy shrugged. "It seems like it's one step forward and two steps back sometimes. But this guy has been calling her, the one we met at that clambake a while back."

Sam looked puzzled for a moment. Then it dawned on her who Darcy was talking about. "You mean Howie Lawrence?"

"Right!" Darcy said. "They've been having this great phone friendship, and then last week Howie came over and we rented a video. Well, now he's asked Molly to the movies, so I wanted to get her something special to wear."

"That is so cool!" Sam exclaimed. She really had to laugh. Howie Lawrence was a nice guy she, Emma, and Carrie had met the summer before. He'd had a terrible crush on Carrie, who hadn't returned his amorous feelings. Well, now it seemed as if Howie Lawrence had a new love interest!

"She hasn't even said she'll go out with him yet," Darcy admitted. "I'm hoping some new killer outfit will help persuade her."

Just then Becky stomped over to Sam. "This store sucks," she said. "You know that sweepstakes they're having where you win a trip to the Bahamas? Well, the salesgirl says we can't enter because you have to be eighteen."

"Enter for us, okay?" Allie asked Sam, coming up beside her sister.

Sam looked over at a huge display with bigger-than-life cutouts of a cute girl and guy, each wearing a bathing suit by Paradise Swimwear. Next to the cutout figures a sign read, *Win a Trip for Two to Paradise.* The Cheap Boutique carried a lot of Paradise's beachwear, and the company was sponsoring the sweepstakes. Other stores all across the country were participating as well. Sam knew this because she'd already read all the information on the entry form when she and Carrie and Emma had entered the week before.

"Sorry, I already filled out a form, and you can only enter once," Sam told her.

Becky took over at Darcy. "Would you enter for me?"

Darcy took in the Paradise display. "Nope, but I think I'll enter for me," she said, walking over to pick up a form.

Becky made a noise of disgust and strode away. Allie followed her.

"That's Becky and Allie for you," Sam explained apologetically to Darcy. "Sorry—they haven't got the best manners in the world."

"I probably don't, either," Darcy said, reading over the entry form. "Well, it says here that all I have to do is fill this out. I can handle that."

"Better do it quick. Today is the last day to enter the sweepstakes," the salesgirl said as she walked over to them. "In fact, the winner is going to be announced tonight."

"Wait a minute," Sam said, her hands on her hips. "How can the winner be announced tonight if there are entry forms all over the country, and no one has collected them yet?"

"There's a hookup to each store's computer," the salesgirl explained. "Each store is supposed to enter all the data by five o'clock this afternoon. Then the company will pick the winner tonight at nine o'clock at the main office of Paradise Swimwear in New York."

"Miss, I'm still waiting for you to ring this

up!" an angry woman yelled from across the store.

"I'm coming!" the salesgirl called. "I wish I could enter," she said to Sam and Darcy. "I sure could use a week in paradise." She sighed and headed for her irate customer.

"Well, I might as well fill it out," Darcy said with a shrug. "Maybe I'll get lucky."

"Hey, I thought you were psychic," Sam teased her. "Can't you just divine whether or not you're going to win?"

"That's the problem with this psychic stuff," Darcy said absentmindedly as she filled out the entry form. "Sometimes I get flashes about things, and other times I'm a total blank."

"So I guess this is one of those total-blank times, huh?" Sam asked.

Darcy looked at Sam thoughtfully. "Maybe . . . and maybe not."

"You mean you know something?" Sam asked, surprised.

"I never know. I just get certain feelings," Darcy explained.

"And?" Sam prompted.

"And I have a feeling someone I know—someone from this island—is going to win something," Darcy said slowly.

"Is it me?" Sam asked breathlessly.

Darcy stared at her intently. "Why . . . yes! Yes! It *is* you!"

"Oh my God!" Sam screeched. "What am I going to win?"

"I see the number five," Darcy said in a throaty voice. "Fifth prize. You'll win fifth prize!"

Sam grabbed an entry form and scanned it quickly, trying to find out just what the fifth-place prize was.

"A T-shirt?" Sam said to Darcy with disgust. "Me and four hundred ninety-nine other lucky winners are going to get a Paradise Swimwear T-shirt?"

"I made that up," Darcy confessed, her eyes dancing. "The truth is, I haven't got a clue."

"Thanks," Sam said sarcastically.

"I really had you going there for a minute, didn't I?" Darcy laughed.

"You did," Sam finally admitted with a reluctant grin.

But for just a moment, Sam, who had never won anything in her life, had believed she might be about to wing her way on an all-expense-paid trip to beautiful, exotic, incredibly expensive Paradise Island in the Bahamas. She'd dreamed of sipping piña coladas by the pool and breaking the hearts of various international playboys. And best of all, she wouldn't have given a single thought to the monsters while she was there.

"Sam, you've got something gross hanging out of your nose," Becky yelled, pointing at her and making a face.

Too bad Paradise Island was just a dream.

TWO

"You look awful. Couldn't you have worn a push-up bra or something?" Diana De Witt asked, critically cycing Sam's bustline—or lack of bustline.

If looks could kill, Diana would die this instant, Sam thought, staring at her arch-enemy. Unfortunately, Diana was also one of thc backup singer/dancers for the Flirts, so Sam had to spend a lot of time around her.

Sam and Diana were backstage in one of the small dressing rooms at the Play Café, getting ready to go on with the Flirts. Emma was late, and Sam was trying to decide if she should start worrying. And now Diana was criticizing Sam's stage outfit.

Sam surveyed her image in the mirror and sighed. She, Diana, and Emma had picked out four different stage outfits together, and this was her least favorite. It featured a red see-through shirt with a red bra underneath, worn with black leather hot pants and red cowboy boots.

The cowboy boots—which Sam lived in, anyway—were the only part of the outfit she liked. While Diana's full bust and slender torso looked sexy in the see-through shirt, Sam thought she herself just looked skinny and flat-chested. Also, red was definitely not her best color. She began to wonder why she had ever agreed to this outfit.

"Sorry I'm late," Emma called, bursting through the door. "Dog got lost and I had to help find him."

Sam looked at Emma enviously. Although her friend was petite and small-busted, in Sam's opinion Emma looked much better in this outfit than she did.

"Whew, it's still pouring out," Emma said, closing her dripping umbrella and propping it up in a corner.

"I'm just glad you're here," Sam said. "Spending time alone with Diana is not my idea of a good time," she added under her breath to Emma.

"I heard that!" Diana called out from her spot in front of the mirror, where she was expertly applying some lip gloss. "All I did was give you a little constructive criticism for the good of the band."

"Oh, please, someone get me a barf bag," Sam snorted.

"Good idea," Diana snapped maliciously. "Why don't you wear it over your head? Then no one will know who those itty-bitty titties belong to."

"Curl up and die," Sam spat at Diana, seething with anger.

"Hey, you two, come on," Emma chided. "We're about to go onstage together. This is a waste of time!"

"Your hair looks awfully flat," Diana told Emma, glancing at her distastefully.

"It's raining out there, Diana," Emma said coolly. "Water does that."

"Well, it looks dirty," Diana said.

"I just washed it!" Emma protested.

"And you need a touch-up," Diana added.

"I don't even color my hair and you know it!" Emma flared.

"Emma, really," Diana chided. "We went to boarding school together. I know for a fact that your hair was a dull sort of brown back then."

"That is a total lie, you rotten little—"

Sam put her hand on Emma's arm. "You're falling for it," she pointed out to Emma, "just like I did."

Emma took a deep breath. If anything, she loathed Diana even more than Sam did.

After all, she'd known her longer. But as often as she vowed not to let Diana get under her skin, it happened time and time again. "You're right," Emma told Sam in a controlled voice. "Neither of us will sink to her level."

Emma and Sam both settled down to making their final preparations before going onstage and pointedly ignored Diana, who smiled a self-satisfied grin into the mirror.

"It's showtime," Carrie said, sticking her head into the dressing room. "You guys look great."

"Thanks," Sam said gratefully.

"Hey, guess what? Graham is going to introduce you. He's just about to go up onstage!"

"I'm really looking forward to meeting him—up close and personal, you might say," Diana purred insinuatingly. "He's very, very hot."

"He's also very, very married," Emma pointed out.

"And about twice your age," Sam added.

"Two minor and boring details," Diana said nonchalantly, licking her lips.

Sam and Emma shared a look. Diana had gone after both of their boyfriends in the past. Was she really about to try to sink her claws into Graham Perry?

Then Sam realized she was getting too caught up in Diana's hype. After all, Graham Perry had been having world-class beauties throwing themselves at him for years, and he was still with his wife, Claudia.

"I would love to see you make a play for Graham Perry," Sam told Diana, "just so I can watch you get shot down."

"Don't be so sure," Diana said, cocking her head to one side. "His little wifey is getting old and boring, you know."

"She's twenty-six!" Carrie protested.

"Exactly," Diana said smugly.

"Hey, time to rock and roll!" Pres said, coming to stand in the doorway next to Carrie. He gave Sam a slow, sexy grin. "You look mighty fine," he added in his soft Tennessee drawl.

"Right back at ya," Sam told Pres. As she crossed the room to kiss him lightly, she shot Diana a triumphant look and tossed her curls confidently. *Take that, you she-devil from hell*, she thought.

The four girls and Pres crowded into the wings along with the other band members. Graham was already onstage, speaking into the microphone to the packed crowd. "These guys have always been great," Graham continued, "but I can't say they've ever been as hot-looking as they are now—although some of you ladies might disagree with that." The crowd laughed and Graham smiled over at the band. "But more important than that, they're really great musicians and fine songwriters. Please welcome to the Play Café . . . Flirting with Danger!"

The Flirts ran onstage, and the girls took their places behind their mikes. Si, their drummer, counted off, and they launched into "Jailhouse Rock," the old Elvis Presley hit.

Everything seemed to go right. The band was on, and they knew it. Since the band had brought in the girls to sing backup, Flirting with Danger had already gigged at the Play Café twice, but just knowing that Graham was watching them for the first time gave them all a super surge of adrenaline. The tune ended to applause and whistles. One song followed another, each seemingly more successful than the last. After two encores, they ran off the stage feeling completely high.

"That was the coolest thing ever!" Sam exulted, hugging Emma.

"That was the most fun I've ever had," Emma laughed.

"You guys were unbelievable!" Carrie cried, running over to them. "I was sitting right by Graham, and he loved it!"

"Really?" Sam asked, grabbing Carrie's arm.

"Really!" Carrie assured them. "He also said that adding you guys was a brilliant move."

"Yes!" Sam yelled, raising her fist in a triumphant gesture.

"Graham just went back to the guys' dressing room," Carrie added.

"Oh my God, oh my God," Sam screamed to Emma, "we're going to go on tour with him! He's going to make us stars!"

Becky and Allie Jacobs walked over to Sam, Emma, and Carrie and said hello.

"So, did you love it?" Sam asked them, filled with confidence.

"Retread," Becky said in a bored voice.

"As in it's been done before," Allie explained, sounding equally bored.

"I mean, I guess it has a certain appeal if you're, like, over the hill or something," Becky added.

"But, hey, some people even listen to Barry Manilow." Allie shrugged.

"How would you two music critics like to walk home in the rain?" Sam asked them sweetly.

"Two cute guys already offered us a ride," Becky said with a sniff, "so we don't need to go with you, anyway."

"You're not going off with two guys you don't know," Sam said.

"For your info, we do know them," Becky said haughtily. "We've talked to them at the country club—Bobby Kingsley and Luke McKinney. They're in college."

Sam sighed. "Do they know you're only fourteen?"

"No, they don't," Allie said. "Why don't you announce it over the loudspeaker?"

"Look, you two wait for me near the front door. I'm giving you a ride," Sam told them.

"We don't have to—" Allie began.

"Emma! Emma Cresswell!" called a voice in the crowd. A slender girl with a brunette bob made her way through the mob toward them.

"Are you Emma Cresswell?" the girl asked Sam excitedly.

"I know you from somewhere," Sam said, "but I can't put my finger on it."

"I'm Martha, the new salesgirl at the Cheap Boutique," the girl said. "Are you Emma? They told me she's in the band, and I remember you from the store."

"I'm Emma," Emma said, stepping closer. "What are you talking about? Who told you I was in the band?"

"Jane Hewitt, at the number you left," the girl said.

"I don't understand," Emma said in confusion.

"I called the phone number you put on your sweepstakes entry form," Martha said. "The national office called while I was doing inventory. You won!"

"Won what? What am I missing here?" Emma asked.

"The Paradise Swimwear trip for two to Paradise Island in the Bahamas!" Martha said excitedly. "You won!"

Emma's jaw dropped. "I . . . what?"

"You won!" Martha repeated. "I was so excited, I had to come over here and tell you myself."

"Wait a minute," Sam said. "You're saying that Emma Cresswell just won a trip for two to Paradise Island?"

"Yes, yes!" Martha screamed. "Isn't it fantastic?"

"I don't believe it," Sam said, turning to Emma. "You only entered the contest with me and Carrie as a joke!"

"Why would it be a joke?" Martha asked. "I'd give my right arm to win a trip like that."

"It's a joke," Sam said slowly, "because Emma here is rich enough to *buy* Paradise Island if she wanted to."

"Sam!" Carrie protested.

"I'm sorry," Sam said, instantly contrite. She knew Emma was embarrassed when anyone talked about how rich she was. But why, oh why did it have to be *Emma* who won? It just wasn't fair!

"Way cool!" Becky marveled. "Hey, how about if you take me and Allie? Since we're only fourteen, we'd count as only half a person each."

"I can't believe this," Emma said, shaking her head.

"Believe it," Martha told her, "because it's true. They'll be calling you tomorrow so you can tell them when you and whoever you're going to take with you want to leave."

"Thanks for coming to tell me," Emma said in a daze.

"No problem," Martha said, waving goodbye.

"I'm really happy for you," Carrie told Emma, giving her a hug.

"But when will I ever be able to take advantage of it?" Emma thought out loud.

"Now, dummy!" Sam cried. "The Hewitts just gave you the next ten days off, remember?"

"Do you think Kurt will be able to get the time off?" Carrie asked Emma.

Emma shook her head, her face thoughtful. "Kurt needs the money from his two jobs too much to take time off. Besides, who says I have to invite Kurt?"

"Gee, silly me, assuming you'd invite the guy you're madly in love with," Carrie teased.

"What if I invited you instead?" Emma asked Carrie.

Sam looked down at the ground, a lump in her throat. *Well, it serves me right for acting like a jealous witch,* she thought. *Emma can take only one person, so of course she'd rather take Carrie.*

"Me?" Carrie squeaked. "You're inviting me?"

"Actually," Emma said slowly. "I'm inviting you and Sam."

Sam's head snapped around. "Say what?"

"I said I'm inviting the two of you to share the prize with me."

"But you only won a trip for two!" Sam pointed out.

"Yes, but as you so rudely pointed out, I can afford it," Emma said with a grin. "Besides, how could I possibly go without both of you?"

"You mean you'd just pay for the third person?" Sam asked.

"You got it," Emma said. "Now will we have a blast or will we have a blast?"

"Am I dreaming?" Sam cried. "Because if I am, I refuse to ever, ever wake up!"

"How are we going to get the time off, though?" Carrie wondered.

"We have to, that's all," Sam said.

"As far as we're concerned, you can have the time off permanently," Allie told Sam.

"Hey, girls, you were great!" Graham Templeton said, walking over to them.

"Thanks," Sam said, grinning at him.

"You know, when I heard the Flirts' new originals, it really made me want to do more songwriting. I never seem to write when I'm here on the island."

"Right," Claudia said, coming up next to her husband and slipping her arm through his. "I hope he'll feel like writing on a great big yacht, though," she teased him.

"I've decided to go out on Billy Joel's yacht with him for a couple of weeks," Graham told them.

"We're all going," Claudia added. "You, too, Carrie. Billy and Graham can write songs, and you and I can loll in the sun with Christie. There'll be two nannies on board for all the kids, so your life will be easy!"

"I'm going, too?" Carrie asked in surprise.

"Consider it a bonus from us, because you're so terrific," Claudia said, kissing Carrie's cheek.

"Oh, that's . . . that's fabulous!" Carrie said wonderingly.

"If you really mean that, what Carrie would like to do instead is to go to Paradise Island with Emma and me," Sam blurted out.

"Sam!" Carrie hissed.

"Emma just won a trip and she invited us," Sam continued, ignoring Carrie.

"Is that true?" Claudia asked. "Would you rather do that than go with us on the yacht?"

"Well, I . . . I . . ." Carrie stammered.

"Hey, don't put her on the spot," Graham said with a laugh. "You know our Carrie prefers jazz. Now, if it were Wynton Marsalis's yacht . . ."

"I'm certainly willing to go with you," Carrie told them earnestly. "It's my job."

"This trip isn't part of your job, honest," Claudia told her. "I mean it. There's a huge staff to look after the kids. If you want to go to Paradise Island, go."

"Are you serious?" Carrie asked incredulously.

Claudia laughed. "Bye-bye!" she sang, waving at Carrie.

"How can I thank you? I mean, this is incredible!" Carrie babbled.

Sam was so happy for Carrie. As determined as she was to try to get the time off from work herself, she really didn't think she had a shot. But at least Carrie would be able to go with Emma.

"Believe me," Claudia continued, "I'm doing you a bigger favor than you know. Ian has talked us into inviting his entire band—all the Zit People—to come with us on the yacht. He says they can't afford to miss the practice time."

"Did . . . did you say Ian gets to bring his band?" Allie asked in a hushed voice.

Claudia and Graham turned to the twins, realizing for the first time that they were there.

"You two are in the band, aren't you?" Claudia said.

"We are! We are!" Becky shrieked. "Are you telling me that we're going on a cruise on Billy Joel's yacht?"

"Ian was supposed to get to tell you himself, but the answer is yes," Claudia said with a smile.

Allie and Becky stared at each other for a moment, then grabbed each other and screamed so loudly that Sam had to put her hands over her ears.

"We're going on Billy Joel's yacht! We're going on Billy Joel's yacht!" they screeched, dancing around.

"Gee, isn't Billy Joel over the hill, musically speaking?" Sam teased them.

"Billy Joel is almost as good as Jim Morrison," Becky said. "Besides, he's married to Christie Brinkley."

"You've *got* to get Dad to say we can go," Allie told Sam, grabbing her arm. "Because I will die if he says no."

"I don't think he'll say no, as long as Ian's parents are going," Sam said. "And yes, I'll talk to him," she added.

"You're the greatest!" Becky cried. She turned to her sister. "Let's go tell everybody!"

"But wait for me—" Sam began.

"We know, by the door," Allie finished. "See ya in a few!"

Carrie watched as the twins ran back into the crowd. "Whew! One minute they hate you, the next minute they love you. It's nerve-wracking!"

"You'll *really* have your hands full with them on the yacht," Sam told Graham and Claudia ruefully.

"Not to worry," Claudia said with a grin. "If I know anything about kids that age, they'll hang out with each other, as far away from us adult types as possible."

"Fortunately, it's a big yacht!" Graham added.

"Listen, tell Dan Jacobs he can call me about the trip if he has any questions," Claudia said. She and Graham waved good-bye and made their way through the crowd.

"Billy Joel's yacht," Sam said wistfully. "I'd like to go on Billy Joel's yacht."

"Uh, Sam, how come you're not jumping up and down?" Emma asked her.

"Because I'm not the one going on the cruise," Sam answered.

"What Emma means is," Carrie said, "hasn't it dawned on you that if the twins are going with Graham and Claudia, you can go to Paradise Island?"

Sam just stood there for a moment, letting what Carrie had said sink in. "That's right," she finally marveled. "But it seems too good to be true."

"It *is* true!" Carrie cried. "It really is!"

"I have to ask Mr. Jacobs first—" Sam began.

"What's he going to do, tell you you have to stay here and watch him date?" Carrie laughed.

"And I don't think he could possibly tell Allie and Becky they can't go out on the yacht," Emma added. "They'd run away from home."

"You're right. You're both right," Sam said. "I have only one thing to add."

"What's that?" Carrie asked.

"*Eeeeeeeeeeeeeek!*" Sam screamed with excitement. Then she grinned. "The monsters had the right idea. It feels much better when you scream!"

The three girls looked at one another, huge smiles plastered on their faces. As if on cue, they all screamed at once, jumping up and down with happiness, too excited to care if they looked moronic.

"One for all and all for one!" Sam shouted. "Paradise Island, here we come!"

THREE

Wow. Paradise Island really is paradise! Sam stared goggle-eyed out the window of the black stretch limousine as it moved unhurriedly along the coast highway. There was sapphire-blue ocean glinting in the afternoon sunshine as far as she could see. Out the other side of the limo, where Emma and Carrie were sitting, she saw towering white building after towering white building, which she knew were luxury hotels.

This is unbelievable, she thought. Everything had worked out so perfectly, she had to pinch herself to believe that it was all real. After calling Claudia Templeton to confirm that the twins really were invited on their trip, Dan Jacobs had readily given his permission for the girls to go. Once that was accomplished, he had seemed glad that Sam wanted to go out of town. Sam suspected it was because it meant he could now bring his latest flame to the house to spend the night, but so what? It worked out for everybody!

Sam had hardly been able to sleep the night before, and now the combination of exhaustion and excitement made her feel giddy. *Did we leave Sunset Island only this morning?* Her mind drifted back to the plane flight they'd taken from Maine to New York, where they changed planes for a hop to Miami. In Miami, they'd caught a commuter jet to Nassau in the Bahamas, where a ferry was waiting to take them to Paradise Island. The ferry jaunt had been as smooth as silk, and a black limousine from the Hotel Paradise was waiting for them at the Paradise Island ferryport. *The limo driver even held up a card with our names on it, so we could find him—and he was wearing a tux!* Sam marveled to herself.

The chauffeur's voice broke into her reverie. "Ladies, Hotel Paradise is just ahead on the left," he said over the limo's intercom. "I'll leave you by the main lobby, where you'll check in. Don't worry about your bags. I'll arrange for them to be delivered to your rooms. They'll be waiting for you there."

Just then the limo turned sharply to the left, then pulled to a stop. Sam looked up at the most luxurious hotel she'd ever seen: the Hotel Paradise.

"Girlfriend," Sam said to Emma, poking her in the ribs as she spoke, "when you win a sweepstakes again, make sure I'm still one of your best friends."

"Me too," Carrie agreed, climbing out of the limo after the driver opened the back door for them. "Look at those gardens!"

Sam swiveled her head around to see where Carrie was pointing. Incredibly lush vegetation and palm trees grew practically up to the front entrance of the hotel.

"Hey, cutie!" Sam heard a voice talking from behind her. She turned around. No one was there.

Then she heard the same voice again. "Hey, cutie!" it cried. Sam whirled around again. It was a parrot, sitting high on one of the garden trees. All three girls burst out laughing.

"I'm planning to break a lot of hearts at this place," Sam said with a grin, heading for the entrance. "I just didn't plan on the first one being attached to a set of wings."

"Let's go check in," Emma said, following Sam into the lobby. "I'm already picturing myself on the beach with a tall glass of iced tea."

"Me too," Carrie piped up.

"Me three," Sam agreed, "only in my case, there'll also be three or four major hunks fanning me with palm fronds."

The girls went into the lobby, which looked to Sam to be about the size of the football stadium at Kansas State University, and only slightly less high. *It must be ten stories tall in here*, she thought, staring straight up.

The registration area was directly ahead of them, and it was a bustle of efficiency. In the middle of the lobby was an open-seating restaurant filled with well-dressed people enjoying cocktails and midafternoon snacks. And one entire wall of the lobby was glass. On the other side of the glass were—could it be?—water and dolphins. Sam stared in amazement. It was like the hotel had brought the ocean right inside!

Emma saw Sam staring, and nudged her. "That's part of the dolphin pool," she said. "I read about it in the brochure Paradise Swimwear sent. Twice a day there's a dolphin show, which you can watch either from in here or from outside."

"I think I'm falling in love with this place already," Sam said, pressing her nose up against the glass. A dolphin with striking markings on its back swam over to her and gently bumped the glass again and again.

When Sam walked down to one end of the tank, the dolphin swam after her.

"This dolphin is following me!" Sam said, laughing.

"It must be a male dolphin," Emma teased her. "You know you're irresistible."

"To parrots and dolphins, anyway," Carrie put in.

"I'm naming this big guy Pres," Sam decided as the dolphin nosed the glass again right in front of her. "In honor of you-know-who."

"I suggest we check in," Emma said, "or else we might find Sam engaged to a fish."

"Hey, Pres here is a mammal!" Sam protested.

"And so are you," Carrie said, sighing romantically. "You two have so much in common."

Twenty minutes later, Sam, Emma, and Carrie were having as much fun in the sitting room of their huge corner suite as kids in a candy store. It was the finest hotel room that Sam or Carrie had ever seen. Even Emma, who had vacationed in the ritziest resorts of the world, was impressed by the luxury.

The sitting room had two entire walls of floor-to-ceiling picture windows that looked out over the breaking waves of the Atlantic, an enormous entertainment center with TV, stereo system, and VCR, a fully stocked wet bar, and a bathroom equipped with both a hot tub and a jacuzzi. Off the sitting room were two bedrooms, each with a king-sized bed.

What's more, Emma had arranged for Sam's room to be next door, attached to the sitting room of her and Carrie's suite by a connecting door.

"Ah yes," Sam said, stretching out on a couch conveniently placed in front of the windows. "If only Allie and Becky Jacobs were here, my life would be complete." The girls cracked up.

"Actually, I don't think I can make it through a day without Lorell Courtland and Diana De Witt," Emma joked.

"And to think I remember when you had no discernible sense of humor," Sam marveled.

"Gee, thanks," Emma said, throwing a pillow at Sam good-naturedly.

"This is unbelievable!" Carrie said, flipping through some of the hotel literature that was on a table in their suite. "This place has everything. Come look!"

Emma and Sam leaned over Carrie and looked in the hotel guidebook. Carrie was right. At the Hotel Paradise there were five restaurants, a disco, two snack bars (one that actually floated in the freshwater pool), and a fully equipped health club. The hotel had over a quarter-mile of private beach-front for its guests, along with equipment for every water sport imaginable. There were tennis courts, an eighteen-hole championship golf course, bicycles and mopeds to use, its own glass-bottomed boat, and shows every night in the hotel's huge cabaret theater. There was also the world-famous Hotel Paradise casino, where the richest and best high rollers came to win and lose fortunes on the roll of the dice and the turn of a card.

"I'm ready for that," Sam said, pointing to a full-color photo of the casino.

"I've never been to a casino before," Carrie said, perusing the brochure.

"Me neither," Sam admitted, "but I'm raring to go!"

"Just be careful," Emma warned. "I've seen people lose thousands of dollars in just a few minutes."

"I'm not people," Sam said. "Besides, I have a feeling I've got a talent for it."

"Based on what?" Carrie asked.

Sam walked over to her suitcase and opened it. She reached into the bottom and pulled out an assortment of books and pamphlets. "Based on the fact that knowledge is power," she answered. "Look—I'm completely ready to break the bank." She spread out the books for her friends to see.

"*How to Win Big at Roulette*," Carrie read out loud, taking one of the books. "*Winning Craps*," she read from another. "Oh, here's my favorite," she said, holding up a book for Emma to see. "*You'll Never Need a Job Again*. Very realistic."

"Don't knock it if you haven't tried it," Sam said, grabbing her books back from Carrie. "I'm gonna study on the beach. Then I'm going to the casino to clean up."

"Where'd you get those?" Emma asked, kicking off her shoes.

"Remember when I disappeared into the bookshop in the Miami airport?" Sam asked. "That's where I found them. It was as if they had my name on them."

"It's not as easy as those books make it sound," Emma said. "If it were, everyone would be rich from gambling."

"I'll be cool," Sam promised, as much to get Emma off her back as anything else. She dropped the books on the dresser and rooted around in the bottom of her overstuffed suitcase. "Aha! Here it is. What do you think of my new bathing suit?" She held up a neon-pink maillot.

"I think it looks like it might be big enough to wrap a sandwich," Emma joked.

"Come on," Sam said, "I can hardly wait to try this puppy on. Martha at the Cheap Boutique gave it to me for half price when I told her I was coming on this trip with you."

"Now, Samantha, be a good girl and take your bag into your own room," Emma ordered in a mock mothering tone of voice.

"Yes, Mom," Sam said, dutifully closing her suitcase.

"Carrie and I will get changed, and we'll meet you down by the dolphin tank in ten minutes," Emma added. "And no kissing that loverboy Pres down in the lobby!"

"Okay," Sam said, picking up her stuff. "No kisses for ten minutes. If you're late, no promises. See you there!"

Exactly ten minutes later, Carrie and Emma walked up to Sam, who was having another glass-impeded chat with her favorite dolphin.

"What can I say? He's crazy for me," Sam said as her friends approached.

"Have you got that teeny-tiny piece of hot-pink material on under that T-shirt?" Carrie asked Sam.

"Yep," Sam answered. "I didn't want to make Pres here too nuts. I was afraid he'd break right through the glass if he saw the suit."

"And to think he's allowed to swim in the buff," Carrie mused comically as they followed the signs to the beach.

On the way, they passed a glittery corridor that led to the Hotel Paradise casino. Even at four in the afternoon, it seemed that there was a constant stream of people going to and from the gambling mecca.

These people must be mega-rich! Sam thought, gaping at the gamblers, who were impeccably dressed in designer sportswear. *They're all wearing a fortune on their backs*, she noted. *They're all dressed like Emma!*

Sam glanced over at Emma. Even now she had on a sheer white linen coverup shot through with the narrowest of gold threads. Sam looked down at her own oversized Sunset Island T-shirt and sighed deeply. *I can learn to fit right in with these people. I know I can*, she thought. *All it takes is determination. This is how I've always dreamed of living!*

"Here's my suggestion," Emma said, snapping Sam out of her thoughts. "Let's hang on the beach for the afternoon, and then have dinner at the seafood restaurant in the hotel."

"Sounds good to me," Carrie said as she

led the way out a revolving glass door to a patio area in front of the beach.

"And then we'll hit the casino," Sam added. "I feel lucky!" She pulled her sunglasses out of her bag just as two incredibly cute, well-tanned guys walked by them in the opposite direction. "Whoa, baby! No wonder they call this place paradise," she hooted, turning around to watch the guys.

"Down, girl," Carrie said, turning Sam back around.

"I *loooove* it here!" Sam yelled, throwing her arms out wide.

The girls made their way onto the beach. It was very different from the beach at Sunset Island—much broader, and with much finer white sand and many fewer seashells. The ocean breakers looked a lot bigger. The beach was dotted with colored umbrellas, under which were small knots of people here and there.

"I wonder where we can get one of those?" Carrie said, pointing at an umbrella.

Just then, a white-uniformed dark-skinned man came up to them.

"Can I help you?" he said in a slight British accent, his teeth shining in the afternoon sun.

Emma nodded. "We'd like to arrange for an umbrella," she said politely.

"You are guests of the Hotel Paradise?" he asked.

"We won a sweepstakes," Sam told him.

"Congratulations," the man said, a slight smile on his lips. "I am Karl. I will be your beach attendant for your visit. Now, what can I get you fine ladies?"

"An umbrella would be lovely," Emma said in her cultured voice.

"Instantly," Karl said. "And towels, and some chaise longues. Would you care for something cool to drink?"

Sam whistled. *This is outrageous!* she thought.

"Three iced teas would be lovely, Karl," Emma said.

"Our pleasure to serve you," Karl said, making a slight bow. "All our guests should be as comfortable as possible here in paradise." He turned and was gone in a flash.

"You are so good at that," Sam told Emma. "You sound like you've been ordering people around—in the nicest possible way, of course—for your whole life."

"That's because she has!" Carrie laughed.

"Hey, don't spread it around," Emma said, nudging Carrie in the ribs.

"What's with his English accent, anyway?" Sam asked, truly puzzled.

"We aren't in America anymore," Carrie

reminded her. "The Bahamas are independent now, but they used to belong to Great Britain."

"Enough geography," Emma said, pulling off her white linen coverup. "Let's go for a swim."

"That suit is fantastic," Sam said, gazing at Emma.

"Thanks," Emma said happily. "I got it at that boutique inside the Sunset Inn." Emma's bathing suit matched her coverup. It was all white, with high-cut legs and a low-cut underwire-bra top. A thin thread of gold wove its way through the material.

"Well, I feel *so* attractive now in my navy-blue one-piece," Carrie said with a sigh, unbuttoning her denim shirt and dropping it to the sand.

"Well?" Sam asked as she pulled the T-shirt over her head and struck a model-like pose for her friends.

"I was right! It *is* just big enough to wrap a sandwich," Emma hooted.

"Hey, my motto is, if you've got it, flaunt it!" Sam decreed.

"You look great," Carrie said. "Believe me, if I had your body, I'd flaunt it, too."

"Yeah, well, if I had your bustline, I'd wear shirts cut down to my navel," Sam retorted, "but you never show off your assets."

"Imagination is everything," Carrie said, wiggling her eyebrows at Sam. "Besides, I'm definitely not the shirt-cut-down-to-my-navel type," she added.

"But we're in paradise," Sam reminded her. "I say we live dangerously!"

Karl walked up to them with three chaise longues and an umbrella in tow. Three enormous, fluffy towels were draped over his arm. He handed each girl a towel and set up their chaises and umbrella.

"Thanks, Karl," Emma said. She turned to Sam and Carrie. "Who's up for a quick swim?"

"I'm parking here to study this gambling book," Sam said, plopping down on her chaise.

"See you later!" Carrie called out, running with Emma toward the ocean.

"Okay, how tough can this be?" Sam murmured to herself, cracking open *You'll Never Need a Job Again.*

"Your iced teas," Karl said, reappearing with three tall, frosted glasses on a tray.

"Thanks," Sam said, taking a glass from the tray. Karl set the others on the small table attached to the arm of each chaise.

Sam sipped at the drink, and inhaled the

aroma of the fresh mint and lemon that floated at the top of the glass.

"'Lesson number one—the mindset of a winner,'" Sam read out loud. She was completely absorbed in the book when a shadow fell over her.

"*You'll Never Need a Job Again,*" read a male voice with an English accent. "I could've written that myself!"

Sam looked up at the guy who had spoken. He had brown hair cut short in the back and long in the front, and his grin showed two cute dimples. He was slender but muscular, and his tanned skin glistened against his bright red surfer jams. The other two guys with him were cute, too, Sam noted swiftly. One was tall, blond, and thin with pale skin and a handsome face, and the other was short and cuddly with curly, longish black hair. And all three of them were smiling down at Sam.

"Does that mean you don't work, or you don't have to?" Sam asked him. "Because there's a big difference."

"Bloody right!" he agreed with a grin, but he still didn't say which answer was correct.

By the time Emma and Carrie got back to the umbrella, the three English guys were lounging on the sand next to Sam's chaise, laughing and carrying on as if they'd all known one another forever.

"We can't leave you alone for an instant!" Emma teased as she picked up her towel to dry off.

"Too true," Sam agreed blithely. She turned to introduce the guys. "This is Trevor, that's Nigel, and over there is Geoffrey. They're here on vacation from London. And this is Emma and Carrie."

"Hello," Emma said, wishing she didn't sound so formal. *I've got to stop doing that!* she scolded herself.

"Hi," Carrie added, smiling back at curly-haired Nigel. *I really like his smile*, Carrie thought.

"England's such a total bore in the summer," Trevor said, brushing his hair out of his blue eyes. "So we thought we'd spend a few days here, then trot off to Miami and then perhaps to New York."

"Although New York can be beastly, too," Geoffrey added with a sigh.

"I understand you're a photographer for *Rock On* magazine," Nigel said, looking at Carrie with interest. "I'm a pretty keen fan of it." Carrie smiled at him.

"Hold on, loves!" Trevor exclaimed. "I've an idea. What if we invite you three ladies to join us for dinner this evening in the President's Restaurant?"

"Smashing idea!" Nigel seconded, looking at Carrie expectantly.

"Right, smashing," Sam agreed, stifling a giggle. She turned to her friends. "Well, isn't it smashing?"

"Fine," Emma replied coolly.

"Sounds like fun," Carrie added.

"Lovely," Trevor said. "We'll meet you in the lobby at, say, eightish?"

"We'll book, of course," Geoffrey, the pale one, added.

"Of course," Emma agreed.

"Well, we're off to play a round of golf," Nigel said, getting up from the sand. "We'll see you later. Come on, lads!"

As soon as they were out of earshot the girls started laughing again hysterically.

"Lads?" Carrie squealed. "God, they're like something right out of an English novel!" She playfully kicked some sand on Sam's foot. "I don't know how you do it, Samantha Bridges," she teased, "but you do it."

"I know," Sam said modestly. "It's a talent."

"Nouveau riche if ever I've seen it," Emma commented drily.

"What does that mean? They're rich but

they haven't had money as long as you have?" Sam demanded.

"It's more their style," Emma murmured, looking down at the sand. She knew she was being a snob and she didn't like herself very much for it. *I'm supposed to have gotten over all that stuff!* she reminded herself.

"Spare me," Sam said, rolling her eyes.

"You're right," Emma conceded. "Ignore what I said."

"They seem nice enough," Carrie said with an easy shrug. "And it'll certainly be an adventure."

"Not to mention the fact that they're buying us dinner," Sam added.

"But all our dinners are being paid for by Paradise Swimwear," Emma reminded her.

"That's right," Sam exclaimed. "I forgot. Well, maybe they'll just give us the cash instead."

Emma and Carrie were too dumbfounded to respond, and Sam blithely buried her head back in her book on gambling.

FOUR

"I suggest we dress to kill," Sam said from her place on Emma's bed. Carrie was in the shower, and Emma and Sam were relaxing before dressing for dinner with Nigel, Trevor, and Geoffrey.

"You actually got some sun today," Emma said, peering at the strap mark left on Sam's shoulder.

"Really?" Sam asked, jumping to look at her reflection in the mirror. Her darkly tanned skin stood out against the stark white of the bath sheet wrapped around her. Sure enough, there were faint markings of slightly lighter skin at her shoulders. "And here I thought I was as tan as a redhead could get."

"You're probably tanner than any redhead *should* get," Emma remarked, reaching for the clear nail polish on the nightstand.

"Hey, I do not have typical redhead skin,"

Sam objected, admiring her tan in the mirror.

"Whew, what a great shower," Carrie exclaimed as she padded into the room. "Later on I've got to try that jacuzzi. And the hot tub."

"I've always thought it would be incredibly romantic to do it in a jacuzzi," Sam rhapsodized, plopping herself down on the bed again. "Music playing in the background, vintage champagne, just Luke Perry and me . . ."

"Dream on," Carrie laughed.

"Maybe Pres down in the dolphin tank would like to be invited up for a little romance," Emma suggested. "Although he'd have a hard time fitting in the jacuzzi with you."

"Sex with a dolphin is a little too kinky for me," Sam said regally.

"Sex with *anyone* is a little too kinky for you," Carrie teased. "You're all talk, no action." She headed back to her own bedroom.

"Don't remind me," Sam sighed. "I'm probably the oldest living virgin in the world."

"I'm two months older than you," Emma pointed out, waving her hands to dry her nail polish, "which means I've got you beat."

"Oh, you're going to do it with Kurt any day now, and you know it," Sam told her.

"Maybe," Emma said with a secret smile.

Sam sat up and stared at her friend. "You didn't do it already and not tell us, did you?"

"No," Emma admitted, "I didn't."

"Well, I should hope not!" Sam said huffily. "You can't keep that kind of juicy gossip from your two best friends!"

"At the risk of changing the subject," Carrie said, coming back into Emma's bedroom and catching Sam's last sentence, "what are you two going to wear tonight?"

"Something incredible," Sam said.

Carrie turned to Emma. "What's appropriate?"

"You'll see a lot of understated, elegant simplicity," Emma said with a shrug. "You know, pastel linens and silks that look plain but cost a mint—that sort of thing."

"Gee, my wardrobe is just teeming with that sort of thing," Carrie said sarcastically.

"Understated elegance is not exactly my style," Sam said, getting up from the bed. "I plan to dress for optimum male attention."

"Meaning short on material, long on skin," Carrie translated.

"You got it," Sam agreed, disappearing into her own room.

* * *

"Well, what do you think?" Sam asked as she waltzed back into Emma and Carrie's sitting room forty-five minutes later. She had on a tiny, sleeveless hot pink Lycra minidress with hot pink high heels, and a hot pink ribbon held her curls up on top of her head. Between the high heels and the high hair, she loomed well over six feet tall.

"Taller than the Statue of Liberty," Carrie opined, staring up at Sam.

"That color is great with your tan," Emma added. "You look sensational!"

"And I might say the same for you two," Sam said, taking in the fully dressed Emma and Carrie. Emma had on a white linen pantsuit with a raw silk vest in the palest rose shade underneath, and Carrie was dressed in a plaid sundress that fell in graceful folds to midcalf. Sam had on quite a lot of makeup, Emma a little, and Carrie none.

"You know, to look at us, no one would believe we're friends!" Sam laughed.

"Vive la différence!" Emma said, picking up her small Chanel clutch purse from the couch.

"We are a credit to babedom everywhere, that's all I have to say," Sam decreed as they walked out of the suite and headed down the hall.

When they got to the lobby Sam immediately headed for the dolphin tank. "Oh, Pres!" she called. The dolphin with the striking markings swam for the glass and bumped noses with Sam.

"Did you miss me, big guy?" she cooed.

"We really have to find her a human-type male," Carrie told Emma, "and I mean fast."

"Well, speak of the devil—I mean devils," Emma giggled, cocking her head toward the three approaching Englishmen.

"Hello!" Trevor called, bounding enthusiastically over to Emma and Carrie. "I say, aren't you ladies looking spiffing!"

"Is that good?" Carrie asked, making a face.

"Jolly good!" Trevor assured her.

"Yes, I'll miss you too, Pres," Sam crooned through the glass.

"She's talking to a fish," Geoffrey said with dismay.

"Pres is a mammal," Emma informed him gravely, "and a close personal friend of hers."

"Shall we go?" Nigel asked Carrie, offering his arm.

Carrie took it, and the two of them led the way as the group strolled leisurely toward the President's Restaurant.

"Harrington, party of six," Trevor told

the tuxedoed maître d' when they reached the restaurant.

They were seated at a semicircular banquette in front of a huge picture window overlooking the ocean.

"Awesome," Sam breathed.

"Totally," Carrie agreed, staring out at the incredible view.

"I do love the way you Americans talk," Geoffrey said.

"Well, you speak rather spiffingly yourself," Carrie laughed as she opened the opulent-looking menu.

"Mmm, this all looks fabulous," Sam said. "I'll have one of everything."

"The lobster is excellent here," Nigel told Carrie, "if you like lobster."

"Love it," Carrie confessed. "It's just that it's always so expensive."

"Not to worry," Nigel said expansively. "Money is no object. We'll both have it."

Everyone ordered their food, and Trevor picked out some wine, which the wine steward brought over for his approval. The steward poured a small amount in Trevor's glass, and Trevor ostentatiously lifted the wine to his lips.

"This will do," he announced, a look of deep concentration on his face.

"Very good, sir," the wine steward said,

and poured the wine for everyone except Emma, who had ordered mineral water.

"I propose a toast," Geoffrey called out, lifting his glass. "To new friendships and, shall we say, international relations!"

"We'll drink to the friendships part," Sam said firmly.

"It'll do for a starter!" Trevor laughed.

Soon the dinner was served and everyone ate heartily. Trevor ordered bottle after bottle of wine, and the guys drank it as if it were water. The drunker the Englishmen got, the more endless, boring stories they told about the boys' school they'd gone to together—evidently they'd known one another their entire lives. Now all three dabbled in the stock market—in between lavish vacations, anyway.

"And then there was the time Nigel here got paddled by the headmaster for breaking curfew with the headmaster's niece, Melanie," Geoffrey hooted.

"She wasn't even a looker, was she, old boy?" Trevor guffawed. "We all thought you were doing her a favor, what-ho!"

"Any port in a storm, lads!" Nigel yelled, which propelled all three of them into cascades of laughter.

"Maybe we could talk about something other than your school days," Sam suggested while the waiter silently cleared their dishes. The food, she had to admit, had been heavenly, but the company left something to be desired.

"Do you ladies dabble in stocks?" Geoffrey asked.

Before any of them could answer that they had no interest in the stock market, Geoffrey was off on an endless story about bull and bear markets and the future of England's economy. It was beyond stultifying. Even well-bred Emma looked ready to dump her water over Geoffrey's head.

"Wow, would you look at the time," Sam finally interrupted in a loud voice.

"The night is young!" Trevor insisted. "What say we have some champagne and then hit the dance floor?"

"Spanking notion!" Geoffrey agreed. "Trip the light fantastic and all that."

"You know, we'd love to," Sam said gravely, "but I have to take my medication."

"Oh, poor kitten," Nigel cooed. "I hope your condition isn't serious."

"Only if I skip a dose or two," Sam said. "Unfortunately I was so excited about seeing you guys that I forgot all three of today's doses."

"My word!" Nigel cried. "What happens?"

"Oh, nothing too bad," Sam assured him.

A second later her head started to loll on her neck and her body began to slip down the banquette.

"She's going into hydrochloride shock," Carrie said urgently, grabbing Sam to keep her from slipping under the table.

"Right," Emma agreed. "We've got to get her up to the room."

"Oh, yes, by all means," Nigel said, hastily moving so that Sam could slide out of the booth.

"Do forgive our rudeness," Emma said as she and Carrie helped Sam from the restaurant.

"But—" Nigel began.

"Ta-ta!" Carrie called back to them.

When the three girls were far enough away from the restaurant to be sure they couldn't be seen, Sam straightened up. "Let's make a run for it!" she whispered, and all three ran toward the casino, laughing so hard their sides hurt.

"That was genius," Carrie gasped to Sam between fits of laughter.

"Hydro-*what* shock?" Emma asked, cracking up all over again.

"It was the first thing that came into my head," Carrie said, tears of laughter in her eyes.

"I just couldn't stand them another second," Sam said. "I had to think of something. God! That sexist story about the headmaster's niece—that guy is a pig."

"Hey, you were the one who said they were nice this afternoon," Emma reminded her.

"I was wrong," Sam admitted. "They were crashing, bloody bores," she added, imitating their accents to perfection.

"I just hope we don't run into them later," Carrie said, peering around the corner nervously.

"Oh, I don't even care," Sam said, tightening the ribbon in her hair. "I say it's time to hit the old casino!" She headed for the door.

"This place is like its own little world," Carrie said wonderingly as they walked through the gaming room.

Loud music from a rock quartet on a stage in the far corner blasted through the casino. Nearby were the sounds of coins clinking in the slot machines and the shouts of adrenaline-fueled gamblers when they hit their number. Bright neon lights flashed crazy patterns on the walls, the floor, their faces.

"I love it," Sam breathed. "I really love it."

Emma and Carrie exchanged looks. They didn't want her to love it *too* much.

"So where do we begin?" Carrie asked.

"We get coins for the slot machines," Sam said.

"But it's a—" Emma began.

"A sucker's game," Sam finished for her. "I know that. My book on gambling says it over and over. But I've always wanted to try it. Come on, we'll only play for a few minutes. Look at it as entertainment."

They stood in line and exchanged ten-dollar bills for quarters, then walked over to the slot machines.

"So how does this work?" Carrie asked.

"See how there's different kinds of fruit showing in each window?" Emma said, pointing to the row of three boxes that at the moment showed a plum, an orange, and some cherries. "You put in the quarter and pull the lever. The fruits spin around. If you get three matching fruits, or cherries in windows one or three with anything else, you win." She pointed to the win chart printed on the machine. "Three cherries is the highest."

"I like this slot machine," Sam said, pulling up a stool behind them. "It's all dollar signs instead of fruit."

"Hey, I won!" Carrie said as the machine spit two quarters out. "This is fun!"

The three girls played for a while, losing more than they were winning, but winning enough to keep going for a while.

"Hey, I just got three wild cards on this machine," Sam called out. "What does that—"

But the rest of what she said was drowned out by the noise that followed—from hundreds and hundreds of quarters belching out of the slot machine.

"Oh my God!" Sam cried, jumping up.

Emma and Carried hurried over, and a crowd quickly surrounded Sam. The coins overflowed from the tray below, and she started scooping them into a plastic bucket.

"How much did I win?" Sam asked in a daze.

Carrie peered at the win chart on the machine. "You just won five hundred dollars!"

"I'm rich!" Sam shrieked, scooping up bucket after bucket of coins. "I knew I'd have a knack for this! I just knew it!"

"Congratulations," came a low voice with a sexy French accent from somewhere behind her. Sam turned around and stared into the bluest eyes she'd ever seen. The rest wasn't bad, either. He looked to be in his mid-twenties, with a baby face and sensuous-looking lips. He wore a perfectly cut tuxedo, and a huge diamond ring glinted on his finger.

"If winning makes you look this way, you must do it more often," the man said.

"I'd love to!" Sam exulted, her eyes shining.

"Allow me to introduce myself," the Frenchman said. "I am Jean-Claude Chantilly." He brought Sam's hand to his lips.

"I'm Sam Bridges, and these are my friends, Emma Cresswell and Carrie Alden," Sam said, dazzled by the Frenchman's suave manners.

"Sam?" he asked.

"Short for Samantha," she explained.

"Charmed," Jean-Claude murmured, inclining his head. "You would like to turn your coins in for chips, yes?" he asked Sam.

"Oh, you mean chips to gamble with?" Sam said. "Yeah, sure."

"Allow me," he said, and snapped his fingers. Instantly two men in dark suits appeared at his side.

"Please turn these in and bring the chips back to us," he ordered, picking up the buckets of coins and handing them to the men.

"Hey, wait a minute!" Sam protested. "Are you pulling a fast one?"

John-Claude laughed. "A fast one? This is a wonderful expression!" He reached into his pocket, took out ten one-hundred-dollar bills and handed them to Sam. "There. This is about twice what you have won, yes? If I am indeed pulling—how do you say?—a fast one, then you will at least make a profit, no?"

"Uh, no," Sam said, staring at the large sum of money sitting in the palm of her hand. "I mean, yes!"

The dark-suited men went off with the buckets of coins, and Jean-Claude threw back his head and laughed. "*Vous êtes très charmante, mademoiselle!*"

"Say what?" Sam asked.

"He said you are very charming," Emma translated.

"*Exactement,*" Jean-Claude agreed, looking at Emma curiously. "Have we met before, *mademoiselle?* You look very familiar to me."

"What a line," Carrie muttered under her breath.

"Actually, we have," Emma said smoothly. Carrie and Sam turned to her in shock. "My mother is Katerina Cresswell. We were your parents' dinner guests at your summer home in Les Vosges three years ago."

Sam stared at Emma. "You actually know him?"

"But of course!" Jean-Claude exclaimed. "I stopped in for only a moment, on my way to the Riviera. *Je me souviens bien que tu as étée très belle et très ennuyée!*"

"Thank you to the first part, and yes to the second," Emma said with a cool smile.

"What did he say?" Sam demanded.

Carrie shrugged. "Don't ask me, I took Spanish."

"Jean-Claude is the son of François du Barry Chantilly and his wife, Claudine," Emma explained. "Friends of my mother's."

"I don't suppose you have a title or anything like that," Sam asked brashly.

"Sam!" Carrie said reprovingly.

Jean-Claude smiled. "It is no matter," he told Carrie. Then he turned to Sam. "As a matter of fact, *mademoiselle*, my father is a *vicomte*—a viscount."

"What's a viscount?" Sam asked.

"Minor royalty, I assure you," Jean-Claude said with a self-deprecating shrug.

"Oh well, as long as it's only minor . . ." Sam said.

Jean-Claude laughed. Just then the dark-suited men returned with Sam's chips.

"There, you see?" he said, his eyes twinkling as he handed her the chips. "I did not pull a fast one."

Sam looked down at the five gold-colored chips in her hands. "Oh yeah? Only five chips?"

"They are worth a hundred dollars each," Jean-Claude explained.

Sam looked closer and saw that he was right. "I knew that," she said with dignity.

"I would love to take you to the blackjack table," Jean-Claude told Sam, staring into her eyes. "Just looking at you will bring me luck."

"Would you excuse us a moment?" Emma broke in smoothly. "We'll be right back."

Emma cocked her head in Carrie's direction and took Sam by the elbow, propelling her away from Jean-Claude.

"Where are we going?" Sam demanded.

"The ladies' room," Emma said, keeping her hand firmly on Sam's arm.

"You could have gone by yourself," Sam groused. "It is so beat when girls have to go to the bathroom together, like they can only travel in packs. It's really—"

"Shut up and get in there," Emma hissed, half pushing Sam through the door.

"What is your problem?" Sam asked, her hands on her hips.

"Sorry," Emma said, "but I had to talk to you privately."

"Is that guy really a viscount?" Carrie asked, "whatever that is?"

Emma snorted. "His family may *think* they're royalty, minor or otherwise, but there hasn't been any recognized nobility in France for a long time. Of course, there are still some pretentious people who insist on using titles like that. His family is extremely wealthy, though."

"Pay dirt!" Sam squealed. "If I marry him, do I become a viscountette?"

"Viscountess, I think," Carrie said.

"I wanted to warn you to stay away from him," Emma said. "I really mean it."

"Why?" Carrie asked.

"Yeah, why?" Sam said petulantly. "He seems really nice. And as you can see, he thinks I'm mondo charming."

"He has a terrible reputation," Emma said.

"Well, so do I," Sam said blithely.

"I mean it, Sam," Emma said. "He's a spoiled playboy used to getting his own way. There was some scandal with a girl in Burgundy that was covered up by his father."

"Aren't you being a little dramatic?" Sam asked, rolling her eyes.

"I don't think so," Emma said levelly.

"Look, he likes me, he's rich, I'm on vacation, what's the big deal?" Sam demanded.

Emma sighed. "You don't understand. A guy like that looks at you, an American girl who he sees as not being of his class, and he's after you for only one thing."

Sam whipped her hair out of her face and stared hard at Emma. "That is a really bitchy thing to say."

"I just know his type," Emma explained, standing her ground.

Sam looked at Carrie. "Don't you think that's bull?"

"I honestly don't know," Carrie admitted. "But I don't think Emma would tell you that unless she thought you could get hurt."

"God, I'm sick of you two acting like my mother!" Sam screamed. She pulled her comb out of her bag and tugged it through her curls viciously, staring at her reflection in the mirror. "For your information," she finally said, "I can take care of myself. And it's just possible that Jean-Claude actually likes me—or is that too difficult for you to grasp?"

"I wasn't trying to hurt your feelings, Sam, honestly—" Emma began.

"Good, then. Don't," Sam snapped, dropping her comb back in her purse. "I'm going back out there to gamble with Jean-Claude. You two can do whatever you want."

And with that, Sam marched out the door of the ladies' room, leaving Emma and Carrie behind.

FIVE

By the time Sam had walked halfway back to where Jean-Claude was waiting, she already regretted yelling at Emma and Carrie. *Why do I do it?* she asked herself. *I've got to learn to control my stupid temper!* But still, she couldn't make herself turn around and go apologize. While one part of her knew that Emma was truly trying to protect her, another part of her felt as if Emma was telling her she wasn't good enough for Jean-Claude. It didn't make sense—Emma was her friend—but that was how she felt.

"Samantha," Jean-Claude said, his face lighting up with pleasure when he saw her. "But where are your little friends?"

"They're not my little friends," Sam snapped. "They're grown women." *Oh great,* she sighed to herself. *Now I'm taking it out on Jean-Claude.*

"Ah, you have the temper!" Jean-Claude said, raising his eyebrows at Sam contemplatively. "This is a good sign in a woman." He took a step closer to her. "You have the fire here," he said softly, touching her red hair, "and here," he said, putting his hand over his heart.

"You betcha," Sam agreed, feeling distinctly uncomfortable.

Jean-Claude smiled. "Well, then, we are an excellent match, no?"

"I wouldn't know," Sam said coolly, taking a step backwards. Suddenly she wasn't enjoying his flirting anymore. It just didn't feel right. On the other hand, maybe this was how European jet-set types always acted. How would she know? She wished she were back in the ladies' room with Emma and Carrie.

"You can take my word for it," Jean-Claude replied, not at all deterred by Sam's response, "or I can prove it to you later this evening." He moved closer to Sam again, so close that she could feel his breath on her cheek. "I can be very, very persuasive."

"Aren't you coming on a little strong?" Sam asked, self-consciously pushing some curls off her face.

"*Au contraire*," Jean-Claude said. "I am simply a man who knows what he wants."

"And do you always get what you want?" Sam asked, standing her ground.

"Always," Jean-Claude said simply. "Now, shall we adjourn to the blackjack table?"

"Gee, thanks, but I've got plans," Sam said, anxious now to get away from him.

"Hi there!" came Carrie's voice from behind her.

Sam turned around quickly to see Emma and Carrie walking over to them.

"Hi!" Sam said, her voice high-pitched with relief. "I'm so glad to see you!"

Emma and Carrie looked confused. Hadn't they been fighting just five minutes earlier?"

"Come on, we're late for that appointment," Sam said, turning Emma and Carrie around by the elbow.

"What appointment?" Carrie asked, totally confused.

"You know, that pressing appointment with, uh, Pres!" Sam said, saying the first name that came to her mind.

"I will see you soon, *chérie*," Jean-Claude called to Sam as she walked away with her friends.

Sam shivered. Something about the way he said it made it seem more like a threat than a promise.

*   *   *

The next morning, it was only the Caribbean sun streaming through the windows of the hotel room that woke Sam. She stretched deliciously in bed, taking in the gorgeous surroundings, and looked at her bedside clock radio. Nearly nine-thirty. Then she saw the note scrawled on a sheet of Hotel Paradise stationery propped up against her bedside lamp.

Sam—

Good morning, sleepyhead. Emma and I have been up for an hour. We've gone jogging on the beach and tried to tempt your dolphin away from you. No luck. But if you're not downstairs by 10:00 to meet us for breakfast in the lobby, we're going to try again. We've got a secret weapon to lure him this time. Dead fish—mmm!

Love, Carrie

Sam laughed when she read this. So they were trying to steal her dolphin away from her, eh? She'd soon put a stop to that! She jumped out of bed, dashed into the bathroom to take a quick shower, and hurriedly put on her new pink swimsuit, a pair of cutoff shorts, and a man's white T-shirt. She scooted out to the elevator, rode it to the lobby, and walked up to Emma and Carrie at their table in the lobby restaurant at the stroke of ten.

"Just testing you," Sam said, sidling up to them. "Stealing my Pres from me? Sure you are!" She sat down and grabbed a fresh-baked croissant from a breadbasket that was filled with all sorts of goodies.

"Well, he was asking for you," Emma said, "but then he started talking about Carrie here—he called her the curvy brunette with the great smile." She took a sip from a teacup.

She looks great, Sam thought, *more relaxed than I've ever seen her. Carrie, too.*

"Listen, I was thinking," Carrie said, downing the last of her coffee. "After last night's adventures with the European contingent, how about if the three of us just hang out together today?"

"What do you have in mind?" Sam asked between bites of her croissant.

Carrie pointed to a brochure on the table. Sam saw that there was a photo of a big boat on it. "I picked this up at the concierge's desk. The hotel has a glass-bottomed boat that guests can go out on. It's called *Heart of Glass.*"

"Nice name." Sam grinned. "If it were

Diana De Witt's boat, it'd be called *Heartless*."

"She's so clever," Emma told Carrie with a wry look.

"What's a glass-bottomed boat, anyway?"

Emma looked up from her tea. "It's a boat that actually has a glass bottom, so you can look down into the water."

"Well, I figured that," Sam said. "What I mean is, what's so interesting about water? Unless, of course, it's filling a bathtub, and Pres is sitting in the tub," she qualified. "Human Pres, I mean."

"The boat anchors above a coral reef," Emma explained. "The glass bottom lets you see all the fish that live around the reef. It's really beautiful."

"Meaning you've done it before," Sam said.

"Well, yes," Emma admitted.

Sam snorted. "Figures. Is there anything you haven't done yet?"

"There sure is!" Carrie laughed. "She hasn't gone all the way with—"

"Forget I mentioned it," Sam said, shaking her head ruefully.

"So, should we go?" Carrie asked.

"Sounds good to me," Sam said, polishing off her third croissant. "These are great!" she added, reaching for a fourth.

"Take it with you, oh bottomless pit," Emma told Sam. "The boat leaves from the ferryport in fifteen minutes."

Sam stood up. "Then we're outta here!" She wrapped her croissant in a napkin and they headed for the lobby.

An hour later, Sam, Emma, and Carrie were sitting in the bow of *Heart of Glass* as it plowed through the slight chop of the Atlantic Ocean. The warm summer wind blew in their faces, salt spray kicked up around them, and gulls and pelicans flew escort overhead.

"Pretty nice," Sam admitted, peeling off her T-shirt to work on her tan.

"Great boat," Carrie chimed in. "And nice crowd!"

"And how!" Sam exclaimed, stretching out. "Did you see that muscular guy with the blue eyes who got on just after we did? What a babeasaurus!"

"I saw him," Carrie said. "He's cute."

"Carrie Alden falls in lust on the *Heart of Glass!* Yes!" Sam grinned as she spoke. "This boat is made to party."

She was right. The *Heart of Glass* was designed for fun. Gleaming white, and more than one hundred feet long, the vessel featured an open bar complete with white-jacketed bartender, a sumptuous buffet lunch, and a DJ spinning island reggae tunes over a primo sound system. And in the center of the boat, down a set of stairs and surrounded by couchlike cushions, was the glass bottom, about thirty feet long and ten feet wide.

They'd been steaming for about twenty minutes when the *Heart of Glass* slowed markedly. The Jimmy Cliff reggae song that had been playing faded out, and the captain's voice replaced it.

"Welcome to the *Heart of Glass*," he said, his voice a mixture of authority and jocularity. "We're here to serve you. Have a good time, and stay safe. You'll notice we've slowed the ship. We're now pulling over Spanish Reef—we'll be anchoring here. We invite you to come to the glass-bottom area to have a look."

"That's our cue," Sam said, standing up.

"So let's go," Carrie added.

The three girls hustled down to the glass-bottom nook and plopped themselves down on a cushion. All the other passengers—about thirty people in all—were filing in, juggling assorted beers, cocktails, and glasses of fruit juice in their hands.

The cute, muscular guy that Sam and Carrie had noticed sat down right next to

Carrie. Sam nudged Carrie in the ribs. "It's fate," she whispered playfully. Carrie nudged her back and rolled her eyes heavenward.

As the *Heart of Glass* slowed to a stop over the reef, the girls looked down through the glass. At first they could see nothing more than rushing water. But as the ship stopped moving, suddenly a wonderful and alien aquatic world snapped into view.

It was as if they were looking down into the biggest aquarium they had ever seen. And it was full of life. Fish were everywhere. The coral reefs themselves reached up almost to the bottom of the *Heart of Glass*.

"Awesome!" Sam breathed. "Look at that!" A big fish that shimmered iridescently with what seemed like a thousand different colors moved into view. It pecked away at the reef nonchalantly.

One of the *Heart of Glass* crew, who wore a nametag identifying him as Timothy, gave a running commentary on the underwater sights.

"That fish with the big teeth, chewing on the coral, is a parrotfish," he said knowledgeably, his accent a pleasant singsong. "See that school of fish down below him, with the black and white vertical stripes?

They're sergeant majors. And the long fish with the big teeth is a barracuda."

The girls watched, fascinated, as the barracuda snapped up another fish with its big jaws and consumed it.

"Must be related to the De Witts," Sam quipped. The girls laughed hard. Sam took advantage of the laugh to lean over and whisper to Emma, "Carrie likes that guy sitting next to her, but she's too shy to do anything about it. Watch this!" she hissed, winking conspiratorially. She then leaned forward and looked right across Carrie at the hunky guy.

"What's your favorite fish?" Sam asked him coyly.

"Excuse me?" the guy said.

"I asked you what your favorite fish is," Sam repeated.

"The guppy," the guy replied with laughter in his voice.

"The guppy, huh?" Sam said. "Well, this is amazing. That's my friend's favorite fish, too." She looked at Carrie and grinned.

"Sam!" Carrie groaned.

"Seriously," Sam continued. "The girl is crazy for guppies."

The guy smiled at Sam and Carrie. "Well, I don't see any guppies down there, but I still wish I had my camera now. This is amazing," the guy said.

"You take pictures?" Carrie spoke up. Photography was a subject she felt totally comfortable with.

"Strictly amateur," the guy said. "How about you?"

"Her name's Carrie and she's a professional," Sam piped up helpfully.

"Sam!" Carrie admonished her. "I can speak for myself!"

"Glad to hear it," the guy said, grinning at Carrie. "I'm Matt Carlton." He stuck out his hand.

"Carrie Alden," Carrie said, shaking his hand. *Strong hands*, she thought. *Nice hands*.

"Are you really a professional photographer?" Matt asked Carrie.

"Oh, no," Carrie told him. "I'm a student at Yale, really, and—"

"Hey, she had some of her photos printed in *Rock On* magazine," Sam interrupted.

"No kidding?" Matt asked. "I'm impressed."

"I just got lucky," Carrie demurred.

"You did not," Sam exclaimed. "Your stuff is great."

"Sam," Emma said in a low voice, touching Sam's arm, "butt out."

"Do you happen to know a writer there named Faith O'Connor?" Matt asked Carrie.

Carrie was stunned. Faith O'Connor was the writer she had worked with when she took photos of Graham Perry at his big concert in Miami the previous winter. She had refused to take shots of him that could prove he was addicted to cocaine, and Faith had practically fired her on the spot. Graham had since completely cleaned up his act. He'd sought counseling and never touched drugs. Carrie's memory of Faith's ruthlessness, however, had remained.

"Yes, I know Faith," Carrie said evenly.

"Well, as far as I'm concerned, she's as big a barracuda as Bubba down there," Matt said, pointing to the huge fish below them. "She'd sell her mother to the devil for the right story."

"I'm glad to hear you say that," Carrie said, relief in her voice. "I had some problems with her myself. So, how do you know Faith?"

"It's a long story," Matt said, running his hand through his sandy brown hair. "How about if you come get a drink with me and I tell you then?" He stood and held out his hand to Carrie to help her up. Carrie took it and they walked toward the bar in the bow of the boat. Sam gave Carrie a big thumbs-up sign behind Matt's back as the two of them walked away.

When they reached the bar, Matt and Carrie each got a piña colada. "So what's the Faith O'Connor story?" Carrie asked.

"Well, I'm an actor and I live in New York," Matt explained. "I was cast in this new play, *Exhaling Darkness*. Nancy Pumpkin, the rock singer, had a part in it, too. Faith decided to do a feature story on our play."

"So what's wrong with that?" Carrie asked, taking a sip of her drink.

"Nothing," Matt said, "if all she had wanted to do was report. But somehow she got the idea that Nancy was having an affair with the director."

Carrie raised her eyebrows quizzically.

"So," Matt continued, "she hounded all of us in the cast whenever she could to try and get the story. She told us all kinds of lies about what Nancy supposedly thought of us and the play."

"That's rotten," Carrie murmured.

"No kidding," Matt agreed. He looked out at the horizon. "Anyway, to make a long story short, O'Connor managed to make everyone so suspicious of everyone else that we all wound up hating one another. She never got us to talk, I'm happy to say."

"Did she ruin the play?" Carrie asked.

"Hard to say." Matt shrugged. "It wasn't a bad script, but there was so much tension in the cast that the whole thing just couldn't come together. It opened and closed in one night," he said wistfully. "But I suppose that's show biz."

"That's terrible," Carrie said, finishing her drink.

"It could have been worse," Matt said philosophically. "At least I got paid Equity scale."

"What's Equity scale?" Carrie asked.

Matt started to explain to her all about Actors' Equity, the union of professional theatrical actors and stage managers, just as Emma and Sam walked up.

"Don't let us interrupt," Sam said. "We're just checking to make sure you two didn't fall overboard."

"These are my friends Emma and Sam," Carrie said, introducing Matt to them.

"Ah, yes, your guardian angel," Matt joked, shaking Sam's hand.

The four of them talked for a while, then Sam and Emma headed back to the glass-bottom area. Carrie and Matt continued talking—about the theater, photography, politics, everything.

He's so easy to talk to, Carrie thought

while Matt was telling her a story about his acting class in New York. *I already feel comfortable with him.*

Before she knew it, two hours had passed and the *Heart of Glass* was pulling back into the ferryport.

"Talk about a fast trip," Matt said, smiling into Carrie's eyes. "I'm sorry it's over."

"It was great talking with you," Carrie said sincerely. "I guess I should go find my friends."

"Wait," Matt said, putting his hand on Carrie's arm. "Can I see you again?"

Before Carrie could open her mouth, Billy Sampson's face swam into her consciousness. Billy. She was in love with Billy. It was bad enough that she had to deal with her old boyfriend, Josh, who was still attracted to her. She just couldn't get involved with yet another guy!

"I don't think so," Carrie said, turning away.

"Are you sure?" Matt asked. "I really . . . well, I'd like to get to know you better."

"I have a boyfriend," Carrie blurted out.

"Is that it?" Matt laughed. "Well, is he here with you?"

"No," Carrie confessed, looking down at the deck.

"Good," Matt said. "Now, you're staying at the Hotel Paradise, right? What room are you in?"

"I really don't think—" Carrie began.

"We'll be friends. That's all," Matt said, gently pushing some hair away from Carrie's face.

"Friends, huh?" Carrie said.

"Friends," he repeated solemnly.

"I'm in room eighteen-oh-four," Carrie told him.

"I'll call you," he promised. He leaned over and kissed her gently on the lips.

The reaction Carrie felt was definitely more than just friendly.

SIX

"Hot fun in the summertime," Sam sang out as they bopped down the hall back to their rooms. Once inside, she threw herself down on the couch near the window. "Whew! I am pooped!"

"Hey, you're getting sand on the cushions," Carrie said, swatting at Sam's feet.

Sam sat up. "You really like that Matt guy, huh?" she asked Carrie.

Carrie shrugged. "He's okay."

"You like him!" Sam whooped. "You know you like him!"

"Okay, I like him," Carrie agreed grudgingly. "But that doesn't mean I'm going to do anything about it."

"Feeling guilty?" Sam asked.

"Leave her alone," Emma admonished Sam, pulling her T-shirt over her head.

"Sam's right," Carrie sighed, reaching down to untie her sneakers. "It's crazy! How can I be so attracted to this guy when I'm in love with Billy?"

"It's really okay, Carrie," Emma said. "You're not married or engaged or anything, you know."

"And you're also on vacation in paradise," Sam added. "Nothing here is real—it's all a big fantasy. Therefore it doesn't count, no matter what you do."

"Oh, is that so?" Carrie said with a laugh. "Meaning calories I eat here won't go to my hips, no matter what?"

"You got it," Sam agreed. "It's magic." She got off the couch and stretched. "I need a shower, and maybe a nap before dinner," she said. Out of the corner of her eye, she noticed that the red light on their phone was blinking. "Hey, you guys have a message," she told them.

Emma sat down in a chair and called down to the desk. "Hello. Is there a message for room eighteen-oh-four, please?" Her face paled and her jaw dropped open. "Are you sure?" she asked the operator. "Yes, yes, I've got it. Thank you." She hung up the phone and sat there.

"Is everything all right?" Carrie asked, going over to Emma.

"You're not going to believe this, but my father is here."

"Here on Paradise Island?" Sam asked.

"Yes," Emma replied faintly.

"But how did he even know you were here?" Carrie asked.

"And what's he doing here?" Sam added.

"I don't know," Emma said, dialing a room-to-room number. "But I'm going to find out."

"Yes?" came Emma's father's voice through the phone.

"Hi, Dad, it's me," Emma said. "What are you doing here?"

"Hey, that's no way for my little girl to greet me," her father chided.

"Is everything all right?" Emma asked, ignoring his remark.

"Sure," her father boomed. "So how's my girl?"

Emma closed her eyes and pinched the bridge of her nose to ward off the headache that was rapidly coming upon her.

"How did you know I was here?" Emma asked her father.

"You left a phone number on the machine at the whatchamacallits," her father said. "The Horowitzes?"

"The Hewitts," Emma corrected him.

"Right," her father said. "Well, I had to stop down here to see a business associate soon, anyway, so I thought I'd come down now and surprise you."

"Well, this is certainly a surprise," Emma said, her head swimming. "Is Valerie with you?" she added, naming her father's much-younger fiancée.

There was silence on the phone. "Valerie and I have parted ways," her father finally said.

"Oh," was all Emma said. She had never liked Valerie, and had let her father know as much in the past.

"Yes, well . . ." her father said, seemingly lost for words. "How about if I take you to dinner tonight? The Salon is the best restaurant on the island—private, can't get in without a special invitation."

"I can't, Dad," Emma said. "I'm here with my two friends, Samantha and Carrie."

"The more the merrier," her father said grandly. "I'll meet the three of you in the hotel lobby at nine. It's formal," he added, "the only place on this island that is. See you then."

"This is so bizarre," Emma said, hanging up the phone.

"What? Tell us!" Sam demanded.

"Well, the good news is he and Minnie Mouse—my almost-stepmother—have broken up," Emma said. "The bad news is, he's taking all three of us to dinner."

"What's bad about that?" Carrie asked. "I was sorry I didn't get to meet him last spring when you went down to Florida to see him."

"This is not a cozy family situation," Emma said with a sigh. She closed her eyes and thought about her feuding parents' seemingly endless divorce, which had only recently been finalized. Much to Emma's mortification, each parent had become engaged to a person in their early twenties.

Frankly, she had a terrible relationship with both of her parents. Her mother was so self-involved, childish, and manipulative that Emma simply couldn't stand to be around her for any length of time. And while she actually kind of liked her father, she didn't really know him very well. He'd always been too busy trying to prove to his wife that he could earn a fortune as well as marry into one, and he'd hardly spent any time with Emma when she was growing up.

Now that she was an adult, he bought her outrageously expensive presents to show his love. And when it suited him, he pretended that they had a real relationship. But Emma found it hard to overcome the reality of the situation.

"Look," Emma told her friends, "you two don't have to go to dinner with us. I'll meet up with you later."

"I don't mind," Sam said with a shrug.

"Neither do I," Carrie insisted. "Besides, you'll need moral support."

Emma smiled at them. "Thanks," she said simply. "Oh, by the way, he's taking us to The Salon. It's formal."

"The Salon?" Sam echoed. "Hot damn! A guy on the glass-bottomed boat told me about it. It's, like, the most exclusive, expensive restaurant on the entire island!"

"Sounds like fun," Carrie said.

"Fun?" Sam screeched. "It sounds to die for!"

"But it's formal," Emma protested. "I didn't pack anything formal. I never thought I'd need it."

"I don't own anything formal," Carrie said with a shrug.

"I don't even know what formal means, exactly," Sam confessed. "If it means an evening gown, the only floor-length thing I own is a hideous mint-green number I had to wear as a bridesmaid in my cousin's wedding."

"Gee, too bad you don't have it with you," Carrie said with a laugh.

Sam shuddered. "I'd go naked first."

"Hey, I've got an idea," Emma said, getting off the bed. "Did you notice that store off the lobby, Cassandra's?"

"The stuff in the window made me drool," Sam said.

"Let's go raid it," Emma said, her eyes shining.

"Emma," Carrie chided, "you know we can't afford that."

"Of course I know that," Emma said calmly. "But my father can."

"Maybe so," Carrie said, "but that doesn't mean he's interested in spending his money on your friends."

"You don't understand my father," Emma said. "We'll be doing him a favor. It'll help assuage his massive guilt about me."

"Sorry," Carrie said, getting up from the bed. "I can't let your father buy me a dress."

"I realize I'm supposed to agree with you," Sam told Carrie.

"Right," Carrie said.

"But if it will really make the old guy happy . . ."

Emma picked up the phone again and dialed her father's room. "Watch this," she told them.

"Yes?" came her father's voice.

"Hi, Dad. I just wanted to tell you that Sam, Carrie, and I didn't bring formal wear, so we're going down to Cassandra's to shop."

"Super," Emma's father said. "Charge it to my room."

"Did you say charge it to your room?" Emma repeated for Sam and Carrie's benefit.

"Of course, sweetheart," Mr. Cresswell said. "I insist."

Emma thanked her father and hung up. "There you have it."

"The shower can wait and the nap can wait," Sam said, slinging her purse over her arm. "Let's go spend someone else's money!"

An hour later, the three girls returned to the room carrying hangers carefully wrapped in plastic with the gold and white logo of Cassandra's discreetly displayed on the upper right-hand corner.

"We've only got an hour before we're supposed to meet my father," Emma said, looking at her watch.

"I'm too excited about wearing this dress to take a nap anyway," Sam said. "See you in a few!"

They showered and dressed carefully, lovingly stepping into their new and extremely expensive evening dresses. Even Carrie decided to wear some makeup for the occasion.

"We're ready," Carrie called into Sam's room. "Come make an entrance!"

"Just a sec," Sam yelled back, putting the final touches on her matte red lipstick. She fluffed her hair one last time and surveyed herself in the mirror. *You fox you*, she told her image. *Now you totally fit in with those high rollers downstairs*.

"Here I come!" Sam sang out, sailing into Emma and Carrie's sitting room.

For just a moment, the three girls stared at one another.

"All I can say is, wow!" Carrie breathed, staring at Sam.

"Ditto to both of you!" Sam cried. "Double ditto!"

They were, to put it plainly, transformed.

Sam had on an emerald-green sheath covered in bugle beads. It was slit high up one thigh and fell in a straight column to the floor. Emma had on a strapless white gown of raw silk that draped to a rhinestone clip at her hip.

But most transformed of all was Carrie. Her usual look was clean-cut and preppy—but not that night. Carrie was wearing a siren-red gown with a sweetheart neck that emphasized her bustline. The waist was tightly fitted, and below that a skirt of red chiffon billowed around her, stopping just above her knees. She was the only one of them who hadn't picked a long gown.

"Carrie Alden, you are one hot mama!" Sam hooted, walking around Carrie in a circle.

"I never owned anything like this in my life," Carrie said, her face shining.

"And you have on actual cosmetics!" Sam added.

"Just some mascara and lipstick," Carrie said with a shrug.

"You've got to have blush with that red dress," Sam said, running back into her room for her blush. She brushed it lightly over Carrie's cheeks. "There," she said, surveying the results. "Perfect."

The three girls stood looking at one another, happy smiles on their faces. "Someone should make a movie about us," Emma said airily.

"And we should play ourselves!" Sam added.

Just then the phone rang. Emma went to answer.

"Hello?"

"Emma? Hi, it's Dad."

"Hi," Emma said. "We're all ready—and we look great, I might add," she said gaily.

"Listen, sweetheart, would you mind very much if I postponed our dinner? I've got a hell of a headache all of a sudden."

"Are you all right?" Emma asked, sitting

down. Her father was not a man who ever gave in to any kind of physical illness.

"Sure, sure," Mr. Cresswell said. "You know me, nothing keeps me down."

But there was a weariness in his voice that Emma had never heard before. What if he was really sick? "Dad?" Emma asked. "Want me to come to your room—or send the hotel doctor?"

"No, no, I just need a nap," her father assured her. "You girls run along and have fun. I'll see you sometime tomorrow—that's a promise."

Emma hung up and turned to her friends. "The big dinner's off. My father isn't feeling well."

"Is he okay?" Carrie asked.

"He says it's just a headache," Emma said, creases of tension appearing between her eyes. "I don't know, though. That just isn't like him."

"Well, maybe he's depressed because he broke up with Minnie Mouse," Sam suggested.

"You don't understand," Emma said. "My father is never, and I mean *never*, sick."

"Do you want to go check on him?" Carrie queried.

Emma stared at the phone, as if she could see through it and into her father's room.

"No," she finally said. "I'm probably overreacting." She got up and picked up her purse. "Let's go down to one of the restaurants—we look too good to stay up here."

"And then let's go gamble with the rich, famous, and snotty," Sam said. "I've still got my five hundred dollars in chips to parlay into a small fortune!"

After a fabulous seafood dinner in a restaurant called Fruits de la Mer, the three girls walked into the casino.

Sam's heart immediately started to beat faster. "I really love it here!" she said with excitement as they walked through the front section, where the slot machines were. "Listen, I really want to try playing roulette. It's over this way."

They stopped in front of a glass-encased wheel, on which numbers appeared surrounded by either black or red. In addition, there were two green spots—zero and double zero. To the side of that was a betting board, with squares showing each number represented on the wheel and various other spots for side bets.

"Could I please turn this in for five-dollar chips?" Sam asked the middle-aged woman behind the roulette table, handing her a one-hundred-dollar chip.

The croupier nodded and pushed twenty pink chips at Sam.

"So, what do you do?" Carrie asked, sitting down next to Sam.

"You put a chip down on a number—or a small group of numbers," Sam said, putting a chip on number thirteen and another between numbers five and six. "And then she throws that little ball bearing into the wheel. If it lands on one of my numbers, I win."

"No more bets," the croupier said, gesturing with her hand over the table.

All three girls watched as the little ball went round and round, finally stopping on number thirty.

"So you lost," Carrie said.

"But I'll win this time," Sam assured them. She placed a chip on thirteen again, and another on the corner of numbers one, two, four, and five.

"That means she has a bet on all four of those numbers," Emma explained to Carrie. "The payoff is much less than if she hits a single number, though."

Two dark-haired men in designer suits came up on the other side of Emma. In a flash they each laid about four thousand dollars' worth of chips on the table.

"No more bets," the woman said.

The ball went around again, and finally dropped—into number thirteen!

"You won!" Emma yelled.

"I did!" Sam said, a huge grin on her face.

The men had lost all their bets. They walked away from the table without a backwards glance.

"Amazing," Carrie said, watching them leave. "They just lost more in ten seconds than I earn working part-time for an entire semester at college."

"Girlfriends, I think I have found my calling in life," Sam said as the croupier pushed two large piles of pink chips over to her. "Why don't you guys play, too?"

Emma and Carrie both exchanged twenty-dollar bills for chips.

"Place your bets," the woman called.

"I'm going for low return, higher probability," Carrie decided, placing three chips so each covered four numbers.

Emma placed two conservative bets and another on a single number.

"I'm feeling luck-luck-lucky!" Sam said, placing four bets, three of them on single numbers.

The girls watched as the metal ball rattled around the wheel one more time, then landed on number seven.

"Number seven," the croupier said. "One winner."

"Whoa, baby!" Sam cried. "I won again!"

An hour later, Emma and Carrie had each gone through their original twenty dollars' worth of chips. Sam, however, was up four hundred dollars.

"Between the four hundred left from winning at the slot machine and all of this, you're up eight hundred dollars!" Emma remarked.

"I suggest you quit while you're ahead," Carrie said.

"Are you kidding?" Sam cried. "I'm on a winning streak here!"

"Statistically, there's no such thing as a winning streak," Carrie said.

"Don't talk to me about statistics," Sam scoffed. "I mean, look at this!" She gestured to her huge pile of chips.

"Well, losing twenty dollars is my limit for the night," Carrie said. "I'm going up to bed."

"Bed?" Sam spluttered. She looked at her watch. "It's only midnight!"

"But I'd like to go snorkeling early in the morning, and I just can't function on no sleep," Carrie told her, getting up from her chair.

"I'll come with you," Emma said. "I want

to check and see if my father called again, anyway."

"Spoilsports!" Sam huffed. "Come on, just a little while longer?"

"Sorry, I'm tired," Carrie said.

"Listen, Sam," Emma began, looking down at the clasp of her purse, "just some friendly advice." She looked back up at Sam. "It's easier to lose than it is to win—so don't go crazy."

"Thank you, Ms. Cresswell," Sam said loftily. "I will certainly keep that in mind."

"You sure you won't come upstairs with us?" Emma asked Sam one last time. "Tomorrow is another day, you know."

"You guys go on," Sam said, waving them away. "I'll be fine."

Carrie and Emma walked away, and Sam turned back to the roulette table. There was no way that either Carrie or Emma could understand how she felt. Carrie was just conservative by nature. And as for Emma, well, she had absolutely no concept of the meaning of money.

Well, for once I've got some money to throw around, too, Sam thought. She placed another bet. *This is only the beginning.*

SEVEN

"Why, Mademoiselle Samantha," a French-accented voice said, "how delightful to run into you."

Sam looked up from the roulette table to see Jean-Claude. The two men who had been with him the day before were standing a pace or two behind him.

"Hello," Sam said. She placed another bet on the table. For the last twenty minutes things hadn't been going very well. She had lost every single bet she'd made.

"I trust you are having a good evening?" Jean-Claude asked.

"Sure," Sam said. She watched the roulette wheel go round and round, finally stopping on her number, twenty-three. *That's more like it!* she thought.

"You are having good luck, no?" Jean-Claude asked.

"Pretty good," Sam said as the croupier pushed some chips at her.

"Place your bets," the croupier called.

"If you would do me the honor," Jean-Claude said, handing Sam a chip.

"You want me to place a bet for you?" Sam asked, surprised.

"I have a feeling you are lucky for me," Jean-Claude said, leaning in close to Sam.

Sam shrugged and reached over to place the chip on the board. Then she saw what was written on it.

"This is a thousand-dollar chip!" Sam squeaked.

"Yes, we start out small," Jean-Claude said, looking at Sam with amusement.

"I can't make a thousand-dollar bet," Sam protested.

"But I insist," Jean-Claude said, putting his hand over Sam's.

She dropped his chip blindly on the roulette table. It landed on number thirty-one.

Immediately the other people at the table covered number thirty-one, and the numbers around it, with their chips.

"See?" Jean-Claude said. "They think you will bring them luck also."

"No more bets," the croupier called.

Around and around the ball went, finally

landing in number thirty-one—then bouncing out again and landing in double zero.

"Oh, no!" Sam cried. "It was on your number and then—"

"It doesn't matter." Jean-Claude laughed. "You mustn't take it seriously."

"I mustn't?" Sam gulped, thinking about his thousand dollars that had just flown out the window.

"No," Jean-Claude insisted. "It is, after all, only money."

"Right," Sam echoed. "Only money."

Jean-Claude looked Sam over appreciatively. "May I say you are looking very lovely this evening. That gown is splendid on you."

"Thank you," Sam said.

"I wouldn't have thought you would own such a gown," Jean-Claude mused. "It is *très chic.*"

"I don't exactly live in jeans," Sam said, her head held high.

"Ah, this I can see," Jean-Claude said, nodding slowly. He held out his hand to Sam. "Would you do me the honor of accompanying me to the poker room?" he asked.

"What's the poker room?" Sam queried.

"A private room where one must be invited to play. The stakes are very, very high. I think you would find it amusing."

"I don't think so," Sam said, taking her hand back.

"But I insist," Jean-Claude said, a charming smile on his face. "You will sit at my side and your loveliness will bring me great luck."

"I don't want to sit at your side and bring you luck," Sam said. "To tell you the truth, it sounds boring."

Jean-Claude threw his head back and laughed. "I was right! You do have the fire!" He leaned so close to Sam that she could see a faint scar on his chin. "I will look for you later, *chérie.* Perhaps you will change your mind." He picked up her hand and kissed it again, then walked away, his silent companions trailing behind.

Sam just sat there thinking for a minute. *Did I not go because I really don't like him, or because I feel insecure around him?* she asked herself. *Actually, it's probably both,* she admitted, and then shook off any thoughts of Jean-Claude so that she could concentrate on roulette.

It was two hours later when Sam looked at her watch. Her heart was thudding painfully in her chest. She glanced at the last four pink chips in front of her. *How did it happen?* she asked herself wildly. She had gone through all nine hundred dollars of her winnings, except for this last measly twenty dollars' worth of chips. *How could I lose so much so quickly?* But just as it had seemed she couldn't lose before, now it seemed that she just could not win.

"Place your bets," the croupier called out, and Sam put her last four chips on four different numbers.

Please let me win, please let me win, Sam chanted to herself.

"Zero," the croupier called. He scooped all the bets off the table. No one had bet on zero. Including Sam.

Sam just sat there, a sick, empty feeling in her stomach.

"Tough luck, huh?" an older woman next to her sympathized.

"Yeah," Sam sighed.

"Listen, I watched you lose a bundle—it can happen to anyone," she said, waving her cigarette in the air. "It's happened to me tons of times."

"Uh-huh," Sam said hollowly. She felt like screaming, *You can afford to have it happen to you tons of times, but I can't!* But she didn't scream, she just sat there.

"Listen, I'll give you a little advice," the woman said. "It never fails. If you keep playing, your luck will change. It's just the odds, you know?"

Sam heard Carrie's voice in her head: *Statistically, there's no such thing as a winning streak.* Well, that had to mean that there was no such thing as a losing streak, either. Which meant that the odds were in her favor to win at least some of her money back.

"Gamblers without heart should stay out of the casino, that's my advice," the woman said.

"You think I can win the money back?" Sam asked the woman.

"Sure!" the woman said. "If you've got the heart to hang in there, that is."

Sam thought about the five hundred dollars' worth of traveler's checks in her purse. It was all the money she had managed to save from her job. She hadn't had any intention of spending it—she'd really brought it along just so she wouldn't feel beholden to Emma for absolutely everything.

Are you crazy? a voice screamed inside her head. *You can't use that money to gamble!*

"I never leave here a loser," the woman said, lighting another cigarette from the stub of the one she had just finished.

"Never?" Sam asked, her eyes taking in the pile of chips in front of the woman.

"Never," the woman said, blowing a puff of smoke out of her mouth. "Can't stand losers."

I am not a loser, Sam told herself firmly. *And I refuse to leave here a loser*. She got up abruptly and walked over to the cashier's window, where she turned in all her traveler's checks for cash. Then she returned to the roulette table, where her seat was waiting.

"Five-dollar chips, please," Sam said in a strong voice, pushing the money over to the croupier.

"That's the spirit," the older woman cheered.

At first Sam started winning again. But then she began to lose. And lose. And lose. She didn't even notice when the older woman left the table, or when another croupier took over. Finally, terribly, she looked down and realized she had only fifty dollars' worth of chips left.

Panic welled up inside her. Her hands shook as she placed the last chips on the board, praying that this time she would win.

But she didn't. She lost. She had lost every penny she had. Tears welled up in her eyes. *Please let this all be just a bad dream*,

Sam thought, her eyes shut tightly. But when she opened them, she had no chips in front of her and no traveler's checks in her purse.

How could this have happened? Sam asked herself as she ran blindly toward the ladies' room. Once inside the safety of a stall, Sam gave herself over to her tears.

"I am completely screwed," she sobbed out loud, ripping off some toilet paper to wipe her face. *How can I ever face Carrie and Emma? I can't!* she thought, tears streaming down her cheeks. *I have totally messed up this time.*

Sam finally stopped crying and came out of the stall to wash her face. Everything seemed hopeless. She fixed her makeup as well as she could and left the ladies' room, ready to go to bed. *I'll figure it all out tomorrow,* she told herself. *Right now I'm just too exhausted.*

"Ah, Samantha. You are still here," Jean-Claude said when Sam headed for the lobby and practically bumped into him.

"I'm just going to bed," Sam said.

"*C'est dommage,*" Jean-Claude replied. "I was hoping we could have just one drink together."

"Look, if you want to know the truth, I'm

not in a very good mood," Sam said with a sigh.

"What is it?" Jean-Claude asked, a look of deep concern on his face.

"I really don't want to talk about it," Sam said, embarrassed to feel the tears welling up in her eyes again.

"But you have been crying!" Jean-Claude said tenderly. "Please, what can I do to help? You are much too lovely to have tears on your face."

He seemed so genuinely concerned, and Sam was so distraught, that she blurted out the truth. "I lost everything!" she cried. "Everything I won, and all my savings."

"Poor child," Jean-Claude commiserated. "How much was this?"

"Nine hundred dollars," Sam admitted, her voice low.

"No, I mean the total amount," Jean-Claude said.

"That *is* the total amount," Sam said, her temper flaring. "Maybe it's nothing to you, but it's a hell of a lot to me!"

"Ah, I see," Jean-Claude said, nodding gravely. "Well, first we must get you some champagne to calm you down." He took her elbow and led her to a pair of overstuffed velvet chairs. Instantly a waitress was there to take the order, and in a moment they had a bottle of excellent champagne in front of them.

"Here," Jean-Claude said, handing Sam a glass of champagne. "It will make you feel better."

Sam sipped at the champagne. It was cold and delicious, but it didn't make her feel any better. "I don't know how I could have done something like that," Sam mumbled, staring down at the bubbles in her champagne.

"It comes, it goes," Jean-Claude said with a Gallic shrug. He reached over and took Sam's hand. "But a young woman as beautiful as you should not have to worry about such things."

"Yeah, well, I do," Sam said flatly.

"It distresses me to see such sadness on your face," Jean-Claude said.

"I don't know why," Sam answered. "You don't even know me."

"*Au contraire*," he murmured. "I feel as if I have known you forever."

Sam raised her eyebrows at him skeptically.

"Perhaps it is just that I wish to know you forever," he added.

"Sure," Sam said. She was feeling very cynical and very depressed. All she wanted to do was to go to bed and sleep for a hundred years. "Thanks for the champagne," she said, getting up. "I really have to go now."

Jean-Claude stood up quickly, so that they were face to face. "But you have not yet heard my idea," he said.

"What idea?" Sam asked.

"You are so sad," Jean-Claude said. "It would be my pleasure to be your . . . how do you say it? Knight in shining armor."

"What do you mean?" Sam asked.

"Just this," Jean-Claude said. "You are feeling bad about losing your money, and I have more money than I can ever use."

"How nice for you," Sam said drily.

"I make you a small proposition," Jean-Claude continued. "For the pleasure of your company in my suite, I will pay you back all the money you have lost, and five hundred dollars more."

Sam stood stock-still for a moment. She wasn't sure she had heard him correctly. "Are you telling me that you'll pay me *fourteen hundred dollars* if I'll go to your suite with you?"

"This is correct," Jean-Claude said. "Your problems would be solved, no? It is so simple."

"Not so simple," Sam answered, brushing some hair out of her face. "What am I supposed to be doing in your suite to earn all this money?"

"Samantha, you are too young to be so cynical," Jean-Claude chided her.

"Oh, really?" Sam asked. "Well, where I come from, the word *proposition* means only one thing—which is exactly what I think you mean."

Jean-Claude smiled. "Samantha, do you really think that a man like me must pay to have his way with a woman?"

Sam looked at his handsome, confident face. "I guess not," she admitted.

"You insult me with your insinuation," he continued. "I am trying to help you, as a friend."

"As a friend," she repeated.

"*Mais oui*," said Jean-Claude. "Look, to prove to you I am honest, I will give you the money." He reached into his pocket and took out a money clip. He peeled off a number of hundred-dollar bills and handed them to Sam.

"What—what are you doing?" Sam asked him, completely taken aback.

"You think I am a liar? This I cannot tolerate," he said, curling her fingers around the money.

"I can't take this!" Sam protested.

"You have insulted me," Jean-Claude said in a hurt voice. "You must take it."

Sam looked down at the money in her hand. Maybe she was reading him all wrong. Maybe she was just feeling defensive because she felt so insecure around him.

"What would we do in your suite?" Sam asked cautiously.

"Drink champagne, look at the view, get to know each other," Jean-Claude responded. He looked at her and continued, "We will not be alone, *chérie*. So you can feel quite safe." Jean-Claude leaned over and whispered something to one of his companions. In only a few minutes, a beautiful blond woman in a lovely gown of pink lace joined them.

"Jean-Claude," she greeted him softly, kissing his cheek.

"Samantha, this is Marie. Marie, this is Samantha," Jean-Claude said, introducing them.

"So you see, it will be all five of us," Jean-Claude said expansively, indicating that his two suit-clad companions were included in the group.

Sam bit her lip in consternation, trying to figure out what to do. *Nothing awful could happen if there's another girl there*, she reasoned. *Maybe he really just wants to help me out. Besides, he's so rich that the money means nothing to him.* "All right," Sam finally acquiesced.

"Delightful!" Jean-Claude said. He took Sam's arm, and the fivesome walked toward the elevators.

Jean-Claude's penthouse suite took up the entire top floor of the Hotel Paradise. It took Sam's breath away.

"This is . . . unbelievable," she breathed, momentarily at a loss for words.

Two of the walls were all glass, offering a panoramic view of the ocean and the starry night sky. All of the furniture was white, beige, or pale rose. A thick white carpet covered the entire floor of the suite. White couches with a faint beige design were situated in the center of the sitting room to form a conversation area. In front of that was a rose-colored marble fireplace. *Who would ever need to make a fire in the Bahamas?* Sam thought irrelevantly.

"Champagne for the ladies," Jean-Claude told one of his associates, who immediately ran to do his bidding.

"Are those guys on twenty-four-hour retainer?" Sam joked, watching the man scurry to the refrigerator in the sumptuous white-on-white kitchen.

"They are convenient," Jean-Claude said

simply. "Come, let us sit and enjoy the champagne."

Jean-Claude poured champagne into their fluted glasses, then lifted his glass for a toast. "To beauty," he said, and gazed into Sam's eyes as he drank his champagne.

"You have eyes like a *petite chatte*," he murmured.

"What's that?" Sam asked.

"A little cat," Jean-Claude said softly, "a beautiful, sexy little cat."

"Thanks," Sam said. She felt very uncomfortable, and looked over at Marie, but Marie was sitting on the other side of Jean-Claude, calmly sipping her champagne.

Be cool, Sam, she told herself. *There's nothing going on here.* But even as she told herself that, she felt as if she was trying to talk herself into believing it. The situation felt creepy, and Sam couldn't stop her hands from shaking a little around the stem of her champagne glass.

"So, don't those guys want some champagne?" Sam asked nervously, indicating Jean-Claude's companions, who were both standing in the kitchen.

"Would you like them to join us, *petite chatte?*" Jean-Claude asked Sam. He dipped his finger into his champagne, and then painted her lips slowly with the sweet liquid. "We will do whatever you like," he said in a low voice.

Sam jumped at the feel of his finger so intimately caressing her mouth. Her glass tipped, and the champagne spilled all over Jean-Claude's starched white shirt.

"*Merde!*" Jean-Claude exclaimed, jumping up.

"Oh, I'm so sorry!" Sam cried, ineffectually trying to wipe the champagne from his shirt. "I'm really sorry. I didn't mean to. I'll pay for it."

Jean-Claude took a deep breath and seemed to regain his composure. "It is nothing, little one," he assured her. "Please excuse me while I go change. I shall return promptly." Jean-Claude kissed Sam's hand, then Marie's hand, and disappeared down a hallway that Sam assumed led to a bedroom.

"Wow, do I feel stupid," Sam told Marie, attempting a weak smile.

"You're new at this, huh?" Marie said, a kind smile on her face.

"Yeah, I don't usually hang out with European jet-set types," Sam joked feebly.

"Jean-Claude is better than most, so you don't really need to feel so nervous," Marie assured her. "He's a decent sort, and he's usually very generous."

"No sugar, Sherlock!" Sam exclaimed. "I'll

tell you the truth—I'm really glad you're here," she confided. "I thought he was bringing me up here alone for you-know-what."

Marie looked nonplussed for just a moment. "What is it you think you're here for?" she asked carefully.

"Well, just to be friendly," Sam said, realizing it sounded incredibly lame even as she said it.

"How friendly?" Marie asked, putting down her champagne glass.

"Not *that* friendly," Sam explained, "if you catch my drift."

Marie smiled. "I catch your drift," she said, nodding. She stared at Sam curiously. "Do you know what I do for a living?"

"Nope," Sam said.

"I'm an escort," Marie said.

Sam thought a minute. "Does that mean what I think it means?"

"If you think it means that extremely wealthy men pay a great deal of money for my company, then the answer is yes," Marie said.

Sam was starting to sweat. She could feel little rivers of perspiration traveling down the back of her beaded gown. "What kind of company?" she asked, even though she already knew the answer.

"Intimate company," Marie replied. "Very, very intimate company."

Sam jumped up from the couch. "But he told me he wouldn't . . . I mean, he told me this wasn't . . ." she stammered, unable to find the right words.

"A man like Jean-Claude is used to getting his way," Marie said with a shrug of her lovely shoulders. "You aren't real to him. You're just a bauble he can amuse himself with." Marie's face was set hard, as if she was fighting giving in to some deep, frightening emotion.

"But you're so beautiful," Sam whispered to Marie, not wanting to believe what she was hearing. "I mean, you don't have to do this."

Marie gave her a sad-eyed smile. "It's not like in the movies, I'm afraid. No rich, perfect prince is going to come along and save me so that we can live happily ever after. Besides," she added, "I'm quite addicted to the money."

"Well, I'm not," Sam said. With shaking fingers she opened her purse and took out all the money Jean-Claude had given her.

"*Chérie!* Sit down! We have only just begun to enjoy ourselves," Jean-Claude exclaimed as he returned to the room and saw her standing with the money in her hands.

"Oh, no we haven't," Sam said. "Your company has made me suddenly ill."

Sam strode to the door, half afraid that Jean-Claude's two silent companions would grab her. But when it was clear that they weren't making a move toward her, she turned around for a parting shot. "Just keep this in mind, you son-of-a-bitch," she seethed at Jean-Claude. "This is one 'little cat' who can't be bought."

Then she threw the money on the floor and marched out the door.

EIGHT

The next morning, Sam pressed her nose up against the glass of the lobby dolphin tank. Pres the dolphin bumped the glass on his side.

"Pres," Sam said, almost whispering, "how could I have been so stupid?" *Stupid to gamble away all my money, stupid not to listen to my friends, stupid to go with that stupid French guy to his stupid room, and stupid to allow myself to be humiliated by him.*

The dolphin answered by continuing to bump his nose against the glass. *He loves me,* Sam thought, *no matter what I do, no matter what I say. Even if he knew what I knew, which is that I tried to hide the truth about Jean-Claude from myself—that he wanted me to go to his room with him so he could sleep with me—even if Pres knew that, he would still love me.* The question was whether or not she could still love herself.

"Hey, you didn't actually go through with it," Sam reminded herself. *Yeah, but you let yourself be led into the situation,* a voice inside responded.

"Shut up!" Sam said, putting her hands over her ears, as if her conscience would listen to her and just butt out. But even though she knew she'd thrown Jean-Claude's money at him and walked out with her head held high, she couldn't help feeling guilty for having gone to his suite at all. *All because I was stupid enough to gamble away all my money,* she told herself. *Stupid, stupid Sam.*

At least she was alone, which was good, because she really did not want to have to face Carrie and Emma. When Sam had awoken late in the morning, there were two notes at her bedside, one from Carrie and one from Emma. Emma's said that she was going to take a windsurfing lesson and then have lunch with her father, and Carrie's said that she was going to spend the morning on the beach with Matt Carlton. They would all meet again in the early afternoon.

Sam smiled when she saw the dolphin was doing flips in his tank for her. She didn't even notice the white-jacketed young hotel employee who had sidled up next to her.

"Uh, miss?" said the fellow, who looked to Sam to be in his early twenties.

"Yes?" Sam responded.

The young man grinned sheepishly, his tight black curls a halo around his handsome coffee-colored face. "My name is Lance Redbourne," he said with the singsong accent typical of the Bahamas. "I'm in charge of the dolphins. It seems one of them has taken a liking to you."

Sam grinned. "It's mutual," she said, looking down at what she was starting to think of as "her" dolphin.

Lance grinned back. "It's quite amazing to see."

"What's his real name?" Sam asked, watching Pres turn lazy circles in the water in front of her.

"Wilson," Lance said. "After the tennis balls. He liked playing with them when he was a baby."

"Wilson! That's a riot!" Sam laughed. "I mean, you have to admit it's a funny name for a dolphin."

"He's an odd duck, er, dolphin," Lance said, looking into the tank. "He took a real shine to Jodie Foster a couple of years ago when she was shooting a movie here at the hotel, but I think he likes you more."

"I'm irresistible," Sam replied, temporarily forgetting her troubles. If only she could just stay here in paradise playing with Pres/Wilson forever!

"Well, that's clearly true enough," Lance agreed. "So, would you like to feed Wilson?"

"Feed him?" Sam echoed.

"Guests aren't really allowed to," Lance told her conspiratorially, "but I think we can make an exception."

"Will you get in trouble?" Sam asked him.

"With the dolphins, I am in charge," Lance said simply.

"You aren't doing this because you like me, are you?" Suddenly Sam felt suspicious that every guy in the place had an ulterior motive.

"I'm offering because Wilson likes you," Lance said shyly.

Sam smiled at him. "Well, then, I'd love to."

"It's feeding time now," Lance said. "Follow me."

Sam followed Lance up a long staircase to the top of the dolphin tank, and then out a door to a platform over the tank outside. When she looked down into the water, not only could she see Wilson and the other dolphins swimming up to the surface, but she could also see a large crowd gathering in the lobby and out on the patio. Evidently, feeding time for the dolphins was a spectator sport at the hotel.

Sam watched as Lance reached into a nearby burlap bag and took out a foot long fish. He held it out over the water. Suddenly, a dolphin—not Wilson—exploded from the water, shot upward, and grabbed the whole fish from Lance's hands, then splashed back down into the pool.

"Ready to try?" Lance said, reaching into the bag and holding out a fish to Sam. Sam nodded agreement. *The way things are going, one of these dolphins is going to grab my arm instead of the fish*, she thought. But she took the fish and held it out over the pool.

A split second later, Wilson leaped from the pool, heading for Sam's fish. But instead of grabbing the fish, he twisted to face Sam, made a happy-sounding squeak at her, splashed down into the water, then leaped up again and took the fish right from her hand.

"A double-pump!" Lance said, laughing. "You should feel honored. He didn't even do that for Jodie Foster. Here, try another."

And every time Sam held out a fish, it was

always Wilson who took the fish. He did an astonishing assortment of tricks to impress Sam and show off for her, finishing with a somersault where he flipped in midair and plucked the fish from her hand on the way down into the pool. Sam laughed with delight.

"You have a future in this business," Lance told her with a twinkle in his dark brown eyes.

"Thanks," Sam said, "it was really fun." They shook hands, and Sam went back into the lobby and headed for the elevator.

"Samantha Bridges!"

Now, who could be calling out my name? Sam thought, her eyes adjusting to the lobby light again after being out in the bright sunshine.

"Sam, over here!" Sam followed the sound of the voice. *Oh my God*, she thought. *Look who it is. It's Mr. Christopher, the choreographer from Disney World. The guy who fired me!*

All the shame and embarrassment Sam felt over getting canned from her first professional dancing job welled up inside of her, piling on top of her shame from the night before.

"Oh, hi, Mr. Christopher," Sam said, trying to pull herself together and not let her emotions show. "How are you?"

"Just ducky," Mr. Christopher said gaily. "Imagine running into you here!"

"I'm on vacation," Sam said, anxious to bring the conversation to an end.

"So, how's your dancing career?" Mr. Christopher asked.

Yeah, like you care, Sam thought. *You fired me for being too original!* But that's not what she said out loud. Before she could stop herself, she was saying, "My dancing is going really, really well. In fact, I'm checking into the possibility of dancing right here at the hotel—there's supposed to be this big Vegas-type revue in the cabaret that I'd be just right for."

"Is that so?" Mr. Christopher asked, an unfathomable look in his eyes.

"Yep, and I heard they need a redhead," she added.

"I don't think so," Mr. Christopher said slowly.

"Pardon?" Sam said.

"I mean, I don't particularly need a redhead right now," he said.

Sam's face burned with embarrassment. "You mean you're—"

"The choreographer for the Vegas revue," Mr. Christopher finished for her. "Exactly."

"Oh," Sam gulped in a small voice.

"I see you improvise stories as well as dance steps," Mr. Christopher said, one eyebrow arched.

"I, uh . . ." Sam stammered, staring at the carpet.

"No hard feelings," Mr. Christopher said gently. "You really are quite a wonderful dancer."

Sam looked up. "I am?"

"Of course you are!" Mr. Christopher assured her. "You'll find your spot one day."

"Thanks," Sam mumbled.

"Now, if you'd like to come see the show tonight, I can put you on the guest list."

"I'm here with two friends," Sam explained.

"Fine," Mr. Christopher replied. "I'll put you down on the guest list as Ms. Bridges, party of three."

"Thanks," Sam said, still extremely embarrassed.

"Well, must run," Mr. Christopher said, looking at his watch. "Ciao!"

Sam waved good-bye and halfheartedly pushed the button for the elevator.

Samantha Bridges, she told herself, *not only are you stupid, but you have an incredibly big mouth.*

* * *

Emma sat quietly at the linen-covered table in the restaurant and looked across at the man who was her father. *I don't know him, and he doesn't really know me*, Emma thought. *So I have no idea what to say. And why do I think that I have to run this conversation, anyway? I didn't ask him to come ruin my holiday.*

She and her father had met outside in the lobby, gone into the restaurant, looked at their menus, and given their orders to a white-jacketed waiter without exchanging more than some mock-pleasant hellos. Then they had sat silently for five minutes, waiting for their plates of broiled grouper and pompano to arrive.

"So, you're feeling better?" Emma asked at last.

"Sure," her father said. "Sorry to ditch you gals last night. Look, I'm not sure if my schedule will allow me to have dinner with the three of you on this trip . . ."

"I'm just glad you're feeling better," Emma said stiffly.

Silence.

"You don't seem exactly thrilled to see me," Mr. Cresswell said with an ironic smile.

Emma avoided looking him in the eye. "Well, it's not as if you've gone out of your way to stay in contact with me," she said, keeping her gaze on another couple in the restaurant. "Then, when I come here on a fun trip with my best friends, you show up. That's not exactly great timing, Dad."

Mr. Cresswell looked sheepish. Emma could see that her words had struck home. *But why couldn't he have realized that on his own?* she thought. *This is a man who made millions of dollars in the financial services industry, but who has no idea how his daughter would feel if he showed up unannounced.*

"I guess you're right," he said quietly. "I shouldn't have come." Mr. Cresswell fiddled with his knife, then put it back down again. "Life is strange, Emma. I guess that's not very profound," he added, "but there you have it."

"I guess," Emma said, distinctly uncomfortable.

"Getting old is a terrible thing," he said suddenly.

"You're not old," Emma replied quickly. He couldn't be old. Not her father, the man who moved mountains, who never even got a cold!

"I know you didn't . . . like Valerie," Mr. Cresswell continued.

"She wasn't good enough for you," Emma said bluntly.

"Well, you didn't really know her," her father said in a subdued voice. "I loved her."

Emma sighed. "I really don't want to hear about this."

"No, I suppose you wouldn't," he agreed. "But I have no one else to talk to."

Don't tell me that! Emma screamed inside her head. *Don't come to me after all these years and expect us to be close! It isn't fair!*

"I find that hard to believe," Emma said lightly, reaching for a slice of French bread from the sterling silver basket.

"It's true," Mr. Cresswell said sadly. "Valerie was my whole life after your mother and I split up."

Anger welled up in Emma. "I'm not your friend, Dad, I'm your daughter," she finally said.

"Well, I guess I deserve that," her father said sadly. He took a sip from his glass of white wine. "I actually don't know you at all, do I?"

"You're right," Emma said. "And I don't know you."

Their waiter finally brought their lunches and placed them on the table, where they sat untouched.

"Maybe . . ." Emma's father began haltingly, "maybe we can begin to get to know each other."

"Maybe," Emma whispered. Tears stung her eyes.

"I'd like that," her father said simply. "I'd really like that."

And slowly, hesitantly, Richard Cresswell, the father who wasn't really a father, began to talk to his daughter who wasn't really a daughter.

It was a beginning.

At that same moment, Carrie and Matt Carlton were standing thirty feet apart from each other, up to their ankles in the warm Atlantic Ocean, vigorously smashing a small, soft blue ball back and forth with wooden paddles.

Kadima was what Matt called it. He'd brought the equipment with him from New York, and he explained to Carrie that it was a very popular game in Israel, where it had been invented. "It's the rage on the beach at Tel Aviv, I understand," he'd said when he introduced her to it.

Carrie had picked it up quickly—it was a lot like racquetball, except instead of hitting the ball against the wall, you hit it to your partner. Now she was confidently whacking the ball back and forth with Matt, even venturing to try an occasional trick shot between her legs.

"Hey," Matt cried after she hit one of these trick shots, "you're some kind of ringer."

"You're some kind of teacher," Carrie shouted back. "Let's take a break. I'm getting tired."

Together, they made their way back up to the beach to the umbrella that Karl, the beach attendant, had brought out to them earlier. Now under the umbrella they found the special picnic lunch they had ordered in a small cooler.

"Mmm," Carrie said, "food for the hungry. Let's see what's in here—two Jamaican beers, sliced smoked salmon, fresh bread, some fruit—"

"That'll do it," Matt said, reaching for one of the beers and cracking it open. "I don't drink these a lot, but somehow today—"

"It's perfect," Carrie finished the sentence for him. *I really like this guy. He's funny, easygoing, gentle, athletic. But I'm taken . . . aren't I?*

Carrie laid her head on Matt's lap contentedly as she ate. Matt cut the salmon into little pieces, put each piece on a slice of bread, and gently fed the tiny open-faced sandwiches into Carrie's mouth. Carrie had her eyes closed, and with the sun beating down on her she felt absolutely happy.

"You have the greatest look on your face," Matt laughed.

"What look?" Carrie asked, too comfortable to open her eyes.

"Like the cat that ate the canary." He popped another tiny salmon sandwich into her mouth. "Or the cat that ate the salmon," he corrected himself.

"Mmm-hmm," Carrie murmured, her eyes still closed.

"Tell me what you think of this," Matt whispered. And instead of putting another tiny sandwich in her mouth, he bent down and kissed her sweetly on the lips.

Wow. I wasn't expecting that, but . . . Carrie reached up and put her arms around Matt's neck. She returned the kiss with enthusiasm. Passion, even. It was a long time before they broke apart with a sigh.

"Yeah," Matt breathed huskily.

"Yeah," Carrie echoed in an equally breathless voice.

He bent down to kiss her again, but she pulled away.

"I can't do this," Carrie said.

"Why not?" Matt asked, stroking her cheek with his fingertips.

"My boyfriend . . ."

"Right." Matt nodded. "The infamous boyfriend."

"Look, Matt, obviously I like you," Carrie said, rising up on one elbow. "A lot, even," she admitted. "But I feel like . . . well, I'm betraying Billy."

"So you can't kiss me anymore?" Matt asked, a gleam in his eye.

Carrie shook her head.

"Does that mean yes, you can't kiss me anymore, or no, you can?" Matt asked.

"I can't . . ." Carrie said. But she knew that her voice didn't sound very convincing at all.

And when Matt bent down to kiss her again, she didn't pull away.

NINE

"Look, kissing this guy Matt is not the end of the world," Emma told Carrie.

"Sleeping with him, yes. Kissing him, no," Sam added helpfully.

It was early evening, and the three girls had just met up in Emma's bedroom. Carrie had told Emma and Sam how confused she was about Matt.

"But why did I even want to kiss him?" Carrie asked despairingly. "I'm in love with Billy!"

"Maybe you're not so ready to be that in love," Emma suggested.

"But I am!" Carrie protested, throwing herself back on the bed. "Maybe I'm just horribly fickle or something. Maybe something is wrong with me."

"God, lighten up," Sam grumbled, checking out the beginnings of a pimple in the mirror. It was hard for her to relate to

Carrie's getting so upset about a few innocent kisses when she, Sam, had really *major* problems. *Problems I'm too chicken even to tell my two best friends about*, she thought guiltily.

Carrie turned to Emma. "You would never do something like this. You're too in love with Kurt, right?"

Emma shrugged. "I made out with that guy at Graham's yacht party last spring. I'm not so perfect."

"But you and Kurt had broken up at the time," Carrie pointed out.

"Well, I just think you're being too hard on yourself," Emma said gently. "Are you going to see him again while we're here?"

"I don't know," Carrie moaned, burying her head in a pillow. "I'm supposed to call his room if I'm free to do something with him tonight."

"Lucky you, you're off the hook," Sam said, plopping down at the foot of the bed. "You'll never guess who I ran into in the lobby."

"Garth Brooks?" Carrie asked hopefully.

"Not even close," Sam answered. "Mr. Christopher, the choreographer from Disney World!"

"The guy who fired you?" Carrie asked.

"Let's just say we had a parting of the

ways," Sam said, grimacing. "Anyway, he's doing the choreography for the big revue here, and we're all on the guest list for tonight."

"That sounds like fun," Emma said.

"Sure," Carrie agreed halfheartedly.

"You want to be with Matt," Emma guessed, nudging Carrie with her foot.

"I can't help it!" Carrie cried. "I can't stop thinking about him!"

"In that case, you should definitely stay away from the guy tonight," Sam advised, "or else see him and go for the gusto!"

"Oh, that's a terrible suggestion," Carrie said, rolling her eyes. "You know I'm not going to sleep with some guy who lives in New York. I'm never even going to see him again."

"Right," Sam agreed. "So why hang out with him and torture yourself? What are you going to do, zone off your body? 'You can touch only above the neck, Matt, babe,'" Sam said, imitating Carrie. "'Well, okay, only above the waist . . . well, maybe—'"

"Stop!" Carrie screeched, throwing a pillow at Sam. "I get your point. So we'll go see this show."

"How late did you stay out last night, Sam?" Emma asked, searching through her makeup case for a nail file.

"Not too late," Sam mumbled, her face turning red.

Emma looked at her. "What happened?"

"Nothing!" Sam snapped.

"Sam, I know that look." Emma pointed at Sam's blushing face. "Did you lose some of the money you won or something?"

"Yeah, something like that," Sam muttered. She bounced off the bed and headed for her room. "I need a shower," she called back to them.

Sam dropped her clothes on the floor and padded into the bathroom, adjusting the shower spray until the temperature was just right. *How can I tell them the truth?* she thought miserably, rubbing shampoo vigorously into her hair.

At first, she talked herself into the idea that she didn't owe them any explanations, and felt relieved. But by the time she'd toweled dry, she had remembered the time when all three of them had kept secrets from one another, and how horrible the consequences had been. She'd vowed then that she owed honesty to her best friends. *Okay, so I can't get out of it*, Sam sighed to herself. She wrapped herself in a large towel and headed back into their suite. Emma and Carrie were no longer in Emma's bedroom, and Sam followed the sound of their voices to their bathroom.

"You guys, I have to talk to you," Sam began.

"And it was so great," Emma was saying earnestly to Carrie as they both lolled in the hot tub that was big enough to seat four. "I mean, my father and I actually started to talk to each other."

Sam removed her towel and sat down next to them in the hot tub. "What'd you talk about?" she asked.

"I was just telling Carrie," Emma said animatedly. "You know how my dad's always been. Well, this time it was different, it really was!"

"I'm glad for you," Carrie said, settling deeper into the warm water. "Mmm, this is glorious."

"What were you saying when you came in, Sam?" Emma asked.

"Oh, nothing," Sam said, losing her nerve.

"You said you wanted to talk to us," Carrie said, her eyes closed and her hair trailing in the water.

"About what we should wear tonight," Sam improvised.

"How about—" Carrie began, but a knock at the door interrupted her. She looked at Emma. "You expecting anybody?"

"Nope," Emma said. "Just a second!" she called, and got out of the hot tub to get her robe. She put it on and went to answer the door.

"Delivery for Miss Alden," said a young man holding a long white box.

"Thank you, I'll give it to her," Emma said, taking the box. She shut the door and carried the box over to the bathroom. "Oh, Miss Alden!" Emma trilled. "Delivery!"

"For me?" Carrie asked, completely surprised. She got out of the hot tub, grabbed her robe, and put it on. Then she undid the bright red ribbon.

"Oh, look at this!" Carrie breathed, staring at a dozen long-stemmed yellow roses. She picked up a small white card that was enclosed. It read: *Yellow roses for friendship, but the last rose is my heart. Dinner? Matt.*

Emma and Sam both read the card over Carrie's shoulder.

"This is so romantic!" Emma cried.

"What does that mean, 'the last rose is my heart'?" Sam asked.

"I don't know," Carrie admitted, "but I'm overwhelmed."

"Hey, there's a vase in the bathroom," Emma said, "with those dried flowers in it. I'll get it."

Carrie lifted the roses from the box. And then she saw it. The last rose, buried in the bottom of the box, was ruby red.

"'The last rose is my heart,'" Sam quoted. "This guy is too much!"

"I can see how you could fall for a guy like that," Emma said softly, bringing the water-filled vase to Carrie.

"But I'm not falling for him!" Carrie protested. "I can't!" She arranged the roses in the vase, the one red blossom standing out starkly from the eleven yellow ones.

"Are you going to call him?" Emma asked her.

"I have to," Carrie said, "just to thank him."

"I have an idea," Sam said, sweeping her hair up into a ponytail. "Why don't you invite him to dinner and the show with us? You'll feel really safe, because Emma and I will be your bodyguards."

"I won't let that beast near you!" Emma promised grandly.

"Gee, thanks," Carrie laughed.

"So what do you think?" Sam asked. "You can decide at the show if you want to be alone with him after that or not."

"You have a brilliant mind," Carrie told Sam, going to the phone to call Matt.

Yeah, Sam thought. *If she knew the dumb*

things I did last night, she wouldn't be calling me brilliant.

Carrie had a brief conversation with Matt, then hung up the phone and turned to her friends. "It's a go," she reported. "I can't say he was thrilled with the idea of chaperones, but he went along with it."

"Cool," Sam said. "The show is at ten, so I suggest we hit the cabaret at nine for dinner. They don't serve food during the show, only drinks."

"You're getting so organized, planning ahead like an actual adult," Emma teased her.

"Yeah, that's me, Miss Maturity," Sam agreed, waving good-bye behind her and heading into her room. *More like Miss Stupidity,* she added to herself, and shut the door firmly behind her.

"Three great-looking women and me," Matt said with a grin when he walked up to them in the lobby a few hours later. "How did I get so lucky?"

"Charm," Carrie told him, returning his smile. She had to stop herself from leaning over to kiss him, that's how attracted to him she was. *What is the matter with me?* she asked herself. *How can this be happening?* Instead of kissing him she took his arm, and the four of them strolled toward the cabaret.

"I say, old girl, how are you feeling?" an English-accented voice asked from behind the group.

They turned around to see Nigel, Geoffrey, and Trevor, dressed in tuxes.

"Oh, I'm fine," Sam said breezily, remembering the dire illness she'd invented when they were at dinner. "Back on the old medication, makes of world of difference."

"Jolly good," Trevor said. "I had a cousin with that disease of yours, you know. Nasty business. Always falling into her pudding."

"Poor thing," Sam commiserated, snorting back her laughter.

"Well, we're off to The Salon," Geoffrey said, fingering his bow tie. "It's the most exclusive place on the island," he added superciliously.

"Have a good time," Carrie said politely.

"Quite right," Geoffrey agreed, and they headed off in the other direction.

"His cousin had my disease?" Sam chortled. "What was it again?"

"Who knows?" Carrie laughed. "I made it up on the spur of the moment!"

The three girls cracked up, and Carrie explained their run-in with the Englishmen to Matt as they walked down the hall.

Just as they approached the maître d' who

stood at the carved double doors to the cabaret, Sam remembered she was on the guest list as a party of three. Only now she was a party of four. She'd have to improvise.

"Hi," she said cheerfully to the maître d'. "Samantha Bridges, party of four. We're on the guest list."

"Let me see," the man said, scanning a list in front of him. "Ah, here you are. But I only have you down as a party of three."

"Really?" Sam asked, looking surprised. "Well, that's a mistake. It's four."

The maître d' checked his guest list again. "It definitely says three people," he told her. "And the show is completely sold out."

"But I'm a close personal friend of Mr. Christopher's," Sam said huffily. "He won't be amused."

"Mr. Christopher is the choreographer, not royalty," the maître d' said drily. "And I have seats for only three of you."

Matt pulled Sam away from the desk. Carrie and Emma stepped over to join them. "Look, you guys weren't expecting me when you got the house seats," Matt said.

"I find it hard to believe they can't fit one more chair at our table," Sam said. "There's no such thing as a three-sided table, unless they've got little triangular tabletops in there."

"Look, it's really okay," Matt said. He looked at Carrie. "How about if I take you out to dinner?" he suggested. "We can go to that reggae club in Nassau I wanted to show you."

"Well, I don't know . . ." Carrie hedged.

"Come on," Matt said, "it's fate!"

Carrie laughed. "All right." She turned to Sam and Emma. "You don't mind, do you?"

"Not me," Emma said.

"Have a blast," Sam added. "And don't do anything I wouldn't do," she added, winking at Carrie.

"Sam, that leaves me open to many experiences," Carrie laughed, and took off with Matt.

Sam turned to Emma. "Well, Ms. Cresswell, shall we?" They approached the maître d' again. "Sam Bridges, party of two," she said coolly.

"Ah, I see we've shrunk," the man said, and escorted them into the cabaret.

"Dang me, as Pres—the human one—would say," Sam breathed, staring at the huge, ornate nightclub.

Small marble tables flanked by red velvet chairs were arranged in semicircular tiers. The front of the stage had a tall arch rising high above it, and the stage itself seemed as wide as a football field. At the moment the elaborate red and gold velvet curtain was closed, blocking any view of its depth. An enormous chandelier hung from the center of the room, and smaller versions hung over each tier of tables. Sam and Emma's feet sank into the plush red carpet as the maître d' showed them to their table.

"Thanks," Sam said when he held out her chair.

"Philip will see to your needs momentarily," the maître d' said with a small bow, and left.

"These seats are max!" Sam exulted. They were sitting right near the stage, in what were among the best seats in the huge house.

"I guess it helps to be a close, personal friend of Mr. Christopher's," Emma laughed.

"Hello, ladies, I am Philip. I will be your waiter this evening," a musical voice said. The girls looked over at their waiter, a very tall, elegantly slender black man in a white tuxedo. "Will you be dining with us this evening?"

"Yes," Sam said, "we will."

"Very good," Philip said. "Can I bring you a refreshment before you dine?"

"Mineral water, please," Emma requested.

"I'll have a Coke," Sam decided.

Philip nodded. "I shall bring your drinks directly, and your appetizers will follow." He walked briskly away.

Sam looked confused. "How can our appetizers follow? We didn't order yet."

"I guess you didn't check out the hotel guidebook too well," Emma said.

"I read part of it," Sam said. "I mean, it was practically as big as a telephone book."

"The cabaret show has a *prix fixe* dinner," Emma explained.

"Meaning?" Sam inquired.

"Meaning that the price of the cabaret show includes a three-course dinner, and the chef chooses the menu in advance. Everyone gets the same thing, except sometimes you have a choice of a few different entrees."

"Bizarre," Sam said. "What if you hate it?"

"You probably won't," Emma said. "It's often done at very elegant, upscale restaurants."

"It sounds more like eating at home, if you ask me," Sam grumbled. "My mom would make meat loaf, which everyone else loved but I loathed, and I'd have to eat it or go hungry."

"Speaking of your mother, how's it going with your parents now?" Emma asked.

Sam shrugged. "We're speaking. I think they're both still freaked out about Susan—my birth mother—but they're dealing."

"Have you heard from Susan?" Emma asked.

"I got another letter from her before we left," Sam said. "Which reminds me, I haven't even—"

"Samantha!" a French-accented voice interrupted her. "So we meet again."

Oh no, Sam prayed, *please don't let it be him.* But she knew before she turned around that the voice could belong to no one but Jean-Claude.

"Hi," Sam said, looking down at the carpet as if it fascinated her.

"Such a coincidence, we have the next table," Jean-Claude said. He gestured grandly to the people with him—his two silent companions, Marie, and another equally beautiful woman. "You were very naughty last night," he scolded Sam.

Sam's face was burning. "I would really like it if you would just leave me alone," she muttered.

"Would you?" Jean-Claude said. There was a nasty edge underneath his surface politeness. "You know, a little girl like you should not play games with a man like me."

"She said she doesn't want to talk to you,

Jean-Claude," Emma said in her frostiest voice. "Why don't you turn around and attend to your guests?"

"Your drinks, ladies," Philip said, setting the mineral water and the Coke on their table.

"We'll have champagne," Jean-Claude told Philip. "Dom Perignon."

"Very good, sir," Philip said, and left.

Jean-Claude turned back to Sam, completely ignoring Emma. "You know, fire can be carried too far, little one. Then it is not so charming, but only stupid," he told her.

Sam kept her back to him and stared down at the tablecloth.

"Jean-Claude, I suggest you shut up," Emma said in a steely voice.

"But I have a score to settle with your little friend," Jean-Claude continued. "Did she tell you that she came to my suite last night?"

Emma looked quickly at Sam, but Sam couldn't meet her eyes.

"Ah, I can see she did not tell you," Jean-Claude said smugly. "Did she perhaps mention that she gambled away all her money?" he continued in that oh-so-polite tone of voice. "And that after she lost, she wanted to be with me so that I would give her all the money she so stupidly lost?"

"This is a damn lie!" Sam said, spinning around to face Jean-Claude. "That's not the way it happened and you know it."

"Is it not?" Jean-Claude asked icily. He turned around to face his party. "Did it not occur just as I described?"

Everyone at the table nodded, even the girl who hadn't been there.

Sam looked at Marie. "You know that's not true!" Sam protested. "You know he tricked me! Tell them!"

"It's just as Jean-Claude said," Marie said quietly, but she couldn't quite look at Sam when she said it.

"You want to play adult games, but then you act like a child," Jean-Claude lectured Sam.

That did it. "Go to hell," Sam seethed, jumping out of her seat. Emma followed.

Jean-Claude got up and stood in front of Sam, his face only inches from hers. "You are nothing more than a little tramp," he told Sam in his casual voice. "But even a tramp must have some standards."

Sam's hand flew into the air and she slapped Jean-Claude across the face as hard as she could. He stood there, the imprint of her hand a red splotch across his cheek.

"How's that for standards?" Sam snapped. She grabbed Emma's arm and together they hurried out of the cabaret.

TEN

"God, Sam, what happened last night?" Emma cried when they reached the hall.

"I don't want to talk about it," Sam said miserably, burying her face in her hands.

"Well, you don't have to, then," Emma said, patting Sam's back comfortingly.

Sam lifted her tear-streaked face and looked at Emma. "He's a damn liar!" she spat out. "He thinks he can say or do anything he wants just because he's rich."

"You're right," Emma agreed. "I'm glad you hit him."

Sam paced around the hall. "I'm not going back into that cabaret. No way. I'll just have to apologize to Mr. Christopher for missing his—"

"Samantha!" Mr. Christopher called, waving frantically to Sam as he practically ran down the hall toward her.

"Damn," she said in a low voice. Then she

quickly wiped the tears from her cheeks and took a deep breath. "Hi, Mr. Christopher," she said, trying for a normal tone of voice.

"I hoped I'd see you," he said, clutching Sam's arm. "I am in a dire crisis."

"Well, I'm, uh, sorry to hear that," Sam said, wondering if Mr. Christopher had lost his mind.

"Five of my girls called in sick in the past two hours. They've got some horrid flu or something," he said, rubbing his temples anxiously. "I've got the understudies ready to go on and every girl moved around to cover, but I'm still short a dancer!"

"Gee, that's too bad," Sam said politely. Somehow at the moment her problems seemed a lot bigger than Mr. Christopher's.

"Then I thought about you!" the choreographer exclaimed. "I realize I'm lost for tonight, but tomorrow night I've got the talent booker from International Cruise Lines coming to check out the show. It's got to be fabulous! If you watched the show with me tonight from backstage and I explained everything to you, could you possibly consider going on tomorrow night?"

Sam's jaw fell open. "Did I hear you correctly?"

"The pay will be a hundred and fifty dollars for the night," Mr. Christopher continued in his frantic voice. "This flu, or whatever it is they have, does seem to be a short-lived bug—some of the others had it earlier—so I'm praying I'll need you to fill in only for the one night."

"B-but—" Sam stammered.

"I know you're on vacation," Mr. Christopher rushed on, "but I'm imploring you . . ."

"This is so sudden," Sam began.

"All right, I'll pay you two hundred dollars," he jumped in. "You must say yes!"

"But how will I learn the choreography that quickly?" Sam asked.

"Dear girl, it's almost exactly same steps I used at Disney World," Mr. Christopher admitted. "The only difference is the sexy costumes."

For the second time Sam was speechless.

"All right, two hundred and fifty dollars for the night," Mr. Christopher said. "That is my final offer."

"I'll do it!" Sam said quickly.

"You're a lifesaver," he exclaimed, hugging Sam.

"Oh, this is my friend, Emma Cresswell," Sam said, finally introducing them.

"Charmed," Mr. Christopher said. "Now, let me hustle you two backstage."

From the wings Sam and Emma watched

the preparations. Some dancers were warming up, technicians were checking lights and sound, and someone was spreading dance resin, a powdered chalk that keeps dancers from slipping, on the stage.

"Let's go back to costumes and make sure the outfits will fit you," Mr. Christopher said.

They walked down a hall and into a huge room full of amazing costumes. Rows and rows of brightly colored costumes divided by type filled the room. There was a section of 1920's-style flapper outfits, then a section of beaded gowns, then some spangled bustiers, and so on.

"Maddie, this is Sam. She'll be filling in tomorrow," Mr. Christopher said, introducing Sam to an elderly woman in a black dress with a starched white collar. "Have her try on all of Sheila's costumes." He hugged Sam again. "I'll be back soon."

"He's awfully huggy for someone who once fired you," Emma whispered to Sam.

"Maybe it's really true—what goes around comes around," Sam said in wonder. "And now I'm saving his butt!"

"So, here you are to save the day," Maddie said. She gave Sam a bright smile that showed a gold tooth.

"I hope so," she answered. *Not to mention*

making two hundred and fifty bucks in one night, she added to herself.

"You look just about Sheila's size," Maddie said, nodding at Sam. "All you children are so skinny!" She took a gold beaded gown off a hanger. "Try this on."

"Here?" Sam said. People kept rushing in and out of the costume room.

"Ain't no one looking at you, child," Maddie assured her. "They're too busy and they don't care, anyhow."

Sam shrugged and pulled the dress she was wearing over her head. Then she stepped into the gown.

"A perfect fit," Maddie said, zipping Sam up.

Sam walked over to the full-length mirror and examined herself. The gown was cut nearly to her navel in the front, with two lines of beading that barely covered her breasts. The slit up her leg came practically to her waist.

"Whoa, this is one hot dress!" Sam exclaimed.

"Thank you, baby. I designed it," Maddie said, helping her out of it.

"You're very talented," Emma told her.

"I do my best," Maddie said with a grin.

Sam tried on five different costumes, each more outrageous than the last. In addition to the gold dress there was a red sequined bustier with a matching G-string, a white gown with a rhinestone-studded halter top, an outfit that would have looked like it belonged on a milkmaid except for its see-through skirt and tiny lace panties that went underneath, and a bikini made entirely of feathers.

"These outfits are just barely decent," Sam told Maddie.

Maddie laughed. "These are showgirl outfits, baby," she explained. "Why do you think they're called that?"

"Because they definitely show a lot of girl," Sam opined, twisting around to see her rear in the mirror.

"Some girls wear a lot less than this," Maddie said, helping Sam out of the feathered bikini and back into her own clothes. "But the show is in fine taste. I even bring my grandbabies to see it."

"Are the costumes a go?" Mr. Christopher asked, rushing over to them.

"She's just Sheila's size," Maddie assured him.

"Marvelous," Mr. Christopher said. "Come along now, we'll watch from the wings."

"Thanks for the fittings!" Sam called back to Maddie as Mr. Christopher propelled her and Emma toward the stage. About twenty girls in gorgeous gowns stood on the stage behind the closed curtain. One fiddled with a strap, another readjusted a sequined headpiece that kept slipping to the side. Two or three looked bored.

"Where's Candy's spot again?" a tall brunette asked in a hushed whisper as she rushed onto the stage.

"Second row, stage left!" Mr. Christopher hissed, his eyes blazing fire. "Understudies," he added in a disgusted tone.

"Ladies and gentlemen," a deep male voice was saying through the sound system, "Hotel Paradise is proud to present *International Girls, Girls, Girls!*"

"Catchy title," Emma murmured sarcastically to Sam as the ornate curtain parted.

Suddenly, the girls onstage each looked ten feet tall. They glowed, they preened, they cat-walked like twenty high-fashion models in their elaborate gowns. The audience oohed and ahhed.

"See how they do a figure-eight pattern on the cat-walk?" Mr. Christopher told Sam. "All you'll have to do at this point is follow the girl in front of you."

After the parade, a quartet of girls came out in multicolored ruffled outfits with bloomers underneath. They looked very old-fashioned . . . except that the corset-like tops ended underneath their breasts.

"Vive la France!" the deep male voice boomed through the sound system. The music changed to a rousing can-can, and the four girls danced energetically, saucy grins on their faces.

Good thing they're all small-busted, Sam thought as the dancers executed a particularly wild jump. *You wouldn't catch me out there dressed—or not dressed—like that for two hundred and fifty dollars, either,* she added to herself.

"Not to worry, your modesty will be strictly preserved," Mr. Christopher told Sam, seeing the appalled look on her face.

Next was "the land of the Arabian nights," as the announcer called it, and six girls did a sinuous dance in harem outfits. Following that was a Spanish number where four girls came out dressed in red sequined toreador costumes with black fishnet tops. They danced with a bull, which was four girls underneath a huge bull's costume.

"You'll be in the next segment," Mr. Christopher told Sam.

Three girls danced out to represent merry Ireland. They were all wearing milkmaid costumes like the one she'd tried on earlier.

"You'll be stage right," Mr. Christopher

whispered. "See where they pair off to do the jig?"

The three girls went into an Irish jig, which was really quite simple. One girl danced by herself—obviously Sam would be her partner the next night.

"It's just a step-ball-change over and over," Mr. Christopher said, "then that little Irishy-looking step with the toe pointed."

Sam nodded. So far the choreography was actually *simpler* than at Disney World!

Sam watched carefully, noting all the numbers she'd be in. Usually it only involved cat-walking around in a sexy costume. A couple of featured dancers did some difficult routines, but Sam wouldn't be in those numbers.

"Okay, here's the big finale," Mr. Christopher whispered forty-five minutes later. "The U.S.A. number, going into the international number."

Sam and Emma watched as twenty girls came out in red, white, and blue costumes. They did a rousing dance number, and Sam concentrated on their combinations. They consisted of exactly the same steps she'd done in the fifties revue at Disney World!

She looked over at Mr. Christopher. "I told you, dear girl," he said with a grin. "Razzle-dazzle 'em!"

Amazing, Sam thought, her eyes glued to the stage. *I could have taught them this routine, I did it so many times.*

The rest of the girls danced out onto the stage in various ethnic costumes, and the big finale was at hand. Once again, Sam recognized the combinations. It was the Disney World Wild West revue!

The show finished to appreciative applause and the curtain came down.

"Well, can you handle it?" the choreographer asked Sam.

"I think so," Sam said.

"Marvelous," Mr. Christopher said, hugging Sam for the third time that evening. "I must scurry—that understudy missed a whole combination in the Mystical Orient number—but I'll see you tomorrow for a rehearsal at, say, two?"

"Fine, I'll be here," Sam promised. She and Emma made their way out the stage door and into the hall.

"Unbelievable!" Sam exclaimed once she and Emma were alone. "He didn't choreograph the majority of that show—he just used what he'd already done at Disney World!"

"At least it means it'll be easy for you to fill in, then," Emma said philosophically.

"Don't you think that show is a piece of

sexist swill?" Sam asked. "I didn't see any guys parading around in sequined jock straps!"

"It *is* pretty obnoxious," Emma agreed. "Want to change your mind about doing it?"

"Hell, no," Sam said. "I'm not one of the dancers baring my hooters. Besides, I need the bucks."

"That's you, Sam," Emma laughed, "pragmatic till the end."

They took the elevator up to the suite. When they got there Emma started to get ready for bed. Sam plopped down on the couch in the sitting room. "What a night," Sam said, staring up at the ceiling.

"Do you want to get some room service?" Emma asked, unzipping her dress as she stood in the doorway of her bedroom.

Sam sat up quickly. "Unbelievable! This is the first time ever that you've gotten hungry before I have!"

"Well, we missed dinner," Emma reminded her.

"I'm really sorry about that," Sam said. She fixed her eyes on the carpet. Now that the backstage excitement was behind her for the moment, all the awful feelings came rushing back. Nothing had changed—except that she wouldn't be completely broke anymore.

"Do you want to talk about it?" Emma asked gently.

"Hey, I guess I *am* hungry," Sam said, dodging the question. "Let's get some really fattening stuff—and insist that a seriously cute guy deliver it."

Emma called down for room service, and then turned back to Sam. "Look, it's okay if you're not up to telling me," Emma said. She slid her feet into her slippers. "I just have a feeling that you really do want to talk about it."

"Well, I do and I don't," Sam admitted. "God, I feel like a total idiot."

"Hey, I'm not asking so that I can judge you, you know," Emma told her gently.

"I know," Sam agreed. Still, it was so difficult for her to admit what a fool she'd been—especially to Emma. *She and Carrie are your best friends*, Sam reminded herself. *And best friends do not lie to each other*. She took a deep breath.

And then she told Emma everything.

ELEVEN

"So that's what happened," Sam concluded in a low voice. "Do you hate me?"

"Of course I don't hate you!" Emma assured her, giving Sam a quick hug. "I've done a million dumb things myself!"

"Yeah, sure," Sam said miserably. "You once belched in public, and have yet to live down the shame."

"Oh, come on, you know I'm not really like that," chided Emma.

"I know," Sam mumbled. "It's just that I feel so stupid."

"It's Jean-Claude who should feel really stupid," Emma fumed. "I'd like to shove one of those expensive bottles of champagne down his smug throat!"

"Well, you warned me about him," Sam sighed, "and I didn't listen—as usual."

"You're being awfully hard on yourself," Emma said. "I mean, you made a mistake gambling more than you could afford—well, lots of people make that mistake. But as far as Jean-Claude goes, you got up and walked out! You didn't do anything!"

"But Emma," Sam said, gulping hard, "somewhere in the back of my mind, I knew he wasn't offering me all that money just for the pleasure of talking to me. I knew, but I wouldn't let myself admit it, because I couldn't face it."

"But you *did* face it, and you left," Emma said firmly.

Just then there was a knock at the door. A handsome young man in a crisp white uniform wheeled in their food.

"Is there anything else I can do for you ladies?" the young man asked.

"Now, that's what I call a leading question," Sam said flirtatiously.

Emma shot Sam a warning look. "No, thank you," she told the waiter, and showed him out of the room. She turned back to Sam. "Good to see you haven't lost your sense of humor."

"Or my appetite," Sam added, pulling the lids off the hot dishes.

The girls ate in silence for a little while, until Sam spoke up. "You know, it's funny," she observed. "I remember I used to play this game with my best friend, Carolyn, when we were, like, twelve or so. I'd say to her, 'Carolyn, would you go to bed with a guy for five hundred dollars?' And she'd answer, 'Never.'" Sam took a sip of her Coke. "So then she'd say to me, 'Sam, would you go to bed with a guy for a thousand dollars?' And I'd say, 'Never!' Anyway, we'd up the ante until we got to about a hundred thousand dollars—or maybe it was a million—and then we both agreed we'd do it."

"Some game," Emma laughed, wiping her mouth with her napkin.

"In our fantasy," Sam continued, "it would take place in a beautiful, luxurious hotel suite—all white and perfect. And the guy would be gorgeous, and in addition to paying us he would of course be madly, passionately in love with us."

"Kind of like that movie, *Pretty Woman*," Emma said.

"Yeah, right," Sam agreed. "I mean, in reality, sex for money is about the most demeaning, degrading thing a woman can do in this world. But in our fantasies, we got everything in one fell swoop—love, money, and happily-ever-after with our handsome prince. It's no wonder little girls are all screwed up!"

"It was completely unreal to you, though,"

Emma pointed out. "You had no idea what sex was even about, except in theory."

"I suppose," Sam agreed, polishing off her cherry cheesecake, "but it's still very messed up."

Emma looked at her watch. "Wow, it's after two."

"Is it, really?" Sam asked, surprised. "Hey, no Carrie!"

"No Carrie is right," Emma agreed. "Should we be worried?"

"I don't think so," Sam said. "Matt seems like a cool guy."

"Appearances can be deceiving," Emma said.

"That's true," Sam murmured, thinking about Jean-Claude.

A key turned in the lock. A moment later Carrie appeared, looking dazed. She sat down heavily on the couch.

"Hi," Sam said. She looked at Carrie closely. "Are you okay?"

"Mmm-hmm," Carrie said, staring at the wall.

"Are you sure?" Emma asked. "Because you look very strange."

"I'm sure," Carrie said in the same weird voice.

"Did you smoke some ganja or something?" Sam asked, using the island term for marijuana.

"Oh, no," Carrie assured them. "Matt doesn't do drugs."

"Well, good for Matt," Emma said. "But did Carrie?"

"No, Carrie did not," she said. "But . . . Carrie had a fabulous, stupendous, incredible time!" She fell back on the couch, her arms flopping wide.

Sam stood over her and looked down. "That's why you're acting so bizarre? Because you had a good time?"

Carrie sat back up. "I am a terrible person," she said seriously.

"We already know that," Emma teased.

Carrie didn't crack a grin. "We went to this reggae club in Nassau," she said, a very serious look on her face.

"And?" Sam coaxed.

"And it was the greatest," Carrie rhapsodized. "We ate fresh fish wrapped in leaves, and fried bananas, and then we danced and danced. There weren't any other tourists there, either," she continued. "Matt knew a Bahamian actor who told him about the place. It was just awesome!"

"So when do we get to the terrible-person part?" Emma wondered.

"I'm coming to that," Carrie said. "We left

there, and we went for a walk on the beach. We talked about everything—it was so easy! So then he kissed me. . . ."

"You slut!" Sam teased.

"And I kissed him back," Carrie admitted. "Over and over and over," she added blissfully.

"So is that what makes you a terrible person?" Emma asked.

"You guys," Carrie said in a confidential voice, "I wanted to make love with him right there in the sand. Things got very hot—I had to tear myself away!"

"Get down, Carrie!" Sam whooped.

"Don't encourage me," Carrie cried. "How could I have done it?"

"But you didn't do it," Emma pointed out.

"I wanted to, though," Carrie confessed.

Sam thought about what had happened to her the night before—how she had thought about doing something, but hadn't actually done it. "Listen, Car, there's a difference between thinking about doing something and actually doing it," she said. "It's not the same at all."

"Right," Emma agreed, shooting Sam a significant look.

"But how can I face Billy?" Carrie moaned. "How can I face myself?"

"Carrie, you didn't sleep with him!"

Emma exclaimed. "You have nothing to feel guilty about."

"But how can I be in love with one guy and get totally hot for another guy?" Carrie wondered.

"Like I told you before," Sam said, "maybe you're just not ready for that kind of love."

"But if I found out Billy did with some other girl what I just did with Matt, I'd be really hurt," Carrie said.

"So don't tell him," Sam suggested.

"I'm not going to," Carrie said glumly. "But I'll still know."

"Look at it this way," Sam said. "Everything here is just a big fantasy. None of it is real—so it doesn't count!"

"I did have fun," Carrie said dreamily, getting up and going into her bedroom.

"Hey, how about we hop in the jacuzzi?" Sam called, going over to the jacuzzi and turning it on. "I'll tell you about our adventure of the evening. I'm going to be a star tomorrow!"

"You could tell her the bad stuff as well as the good stuff," Emma suggested as she padded over to join Sam.

"Well, okay," Sam agreed, stepping into the water. "But only because the ending is so incredibly cool!"

After a long soak and a long conversation, Sam said good night and went into her own room. She lay down on the bed, thinking about everything that had happened. She felt so much better now that she had told her best friends the truth. *Emma and Carrie are such great friends*, Sam reflected. *They really feel like family. . . .*

Family. Sam sat up. She'd never opened the last letter from her birth mother. *Now why was that? I guess it's because I feel closer to Emma and Carrie than I do to her*, Sam realized. *I don't even know her. And . . . well, I guess the truth is that I resent her for giving me up for adoption.*

Sam went over to her huge purse and pushed her hand into the bottom, coming up with the now-crumpled letter from Susan. She slit open the envelope and pulled out the letter.

Dear Sam,

I hope everything is going great on Sunset Island.

I've been editing a new children's book, and the baby had a bad cold, so as usual I've been incredibly busy. I think about you so often, Sam, and really want the chance to make you a part of our family. Now that everyone knows you're in my life—including my husband—I'm hoping that that is possible. I want to invite you to come visit us here in California as soon as you can. If you agree, I'll send you the round-trip plane ticket.

I think you've got the makings of a real California girl.

Love, Susan

Sam stared at the letter until it blurred in front of her eyes. Susan wanted her to visit California. She wanted Sam to become a part of her family. Did she want to go? What would it be like, meeting Susan's husband, who had forced Susan to give her up for adoption, meeting her older brother and baby sister?

"I can't deal with it," Sam said out loud, stuffing the letter back into her purse. She got back into bed and snuggled into the pillow. She sighed deeply. Just like Carrie was with Matt, she was completely of two minds. How could she want to accept Susan's invitation so badly, and not want to, at exactly the same time?

"Break a leg," Carrie said warmly, hugging Sam before she went backstage the next night.

"Break both legs," Emma laughed, adding her hug to Carrie's. "You're going to be fabulous."

"I hope so," Sam said, biting her lip nervously.

"We'll be the ones in the front whistling at the talented redhead." Carrie smiled at Sam, then she and Emma waved good-bye and headed into the cabaret.

"Sam, good, right on time," Mr. Christopher chirped, taking Sam's arm proprietarily. "Let's get you into your first costume."

Before Sam had time to think about it, the show was about to start. Her heart thudded in her chest as she stood there behind the heavy curtain, Mr. Christopher giving her a thumbs-up sign from the wings.

"Ladies and gentlemen, the Hotel Paradise is proud to present *International Girls, Girls, Girls!*"

The curtain rose, and Sam smiled her most dazzling smile. She swept across the stage, following the girl in front of her in the figure-eight pattern she'd seen the night before.

After the opening number, the whole show seemed to pass in a blur. Maddie and an assistant helped her change from costume to costume. Mr. Christopher was always fluttering around, pushing or pulling her into the right spot. Except for one missed sequence during the Irish segment, when Sam went left and everyone else went right, everything seemed to work out.

"You're doing great, baby," Maddie encouraged her, zipping her into the white gown for the All-American number, leading into the big finale.

"Thanks," Sam gasped, and ran into place just as the music began.

Just as if she were still dancing at Disney World, all the moves came back to her. She turned and whirled, dipping and swaying to the upbeat music. As one of the featured dancers took her solo, Sam stood tall, just right of center stage. Even with the bright lights in her eyes, she could make out the front row of tables. And there were Carrie and Emma, grinning up at her.

Somehow, seeing them out there rooting for her made Sam want to dance better than she'd ever danced before. She held her head even higher and shot her legs up in the air into high kicks that seemed to extend to the faraway ceiling of the stage.

And it felt so good! The lights, the audience, her body moving perfectly to the music. *This is where I was born to be*, Sam exulted to herself, moving into a double pirouette. *I really do want a career as a dancer. And I really do believe I can make it!*

As the other girls moved onto the stage for the big finale, Sam gave herself up to the moves she remembered so well from Disney World. She went into the final combination and raised her arms high on the final beat of the music.

The applause washed over Sam, and she grinned hugely. In the front, Carrie and Emma were clapping wildly. Carrie was hooting, and even ladylike Emma was attempting to whistle with two fingers in her mouth!

Sam changed quickly, hugging Maddie and receiving yet another giant hug from Mr. Christopher.

"Samantha, my dear, you came through for me with flying colors," he said, handing Sam an envelope. "Here's your check. You earned it."

"Thanks for the opportunity," Sam said. She paused, then added, "After what happened, I was kind of surprised . . ."

Mr. Christopher took Sam by the shoulders. "Perhaps I didn't make myself quite clear when I let you go back at Disney World," he said. "You have talent, Sam. Major talent. I grant that you lack discipline and maturity, but that you can acquire." He stared into her eyes. "But the gift, that's something you were born with. It's in the genes. Now, it's totally up to you to decide how to use it."

"Thanks," Sam whispered. "I'll remember that."

"You were incredible!" Carrie whooped when Sam came out of the stage door. She threw her arms around her.

"You were the best, honestly," Emma added warmly.

"It was so much fun!" Sam exclaimed. "Did you notice when I screwed up that Irish thing?" she asked them. "All of a sudden the other girl was going one way and I—"

"I assure you, you were perfection," a French-accented voice said from behind Sam.

Oh, no, Sam thought with dread. *I'd know that slimy voice anywhere.*

"Let's get out of here," Sam told Carrie and Emma. Even though Jean-Claude was standing right in front of her, Marie on his arm, Sam looked right past him. She had absolutely nothing to say to Jean-Claude. Ever.

"Excuse me for interrupting," Jean-Claude said smoothly. "I did not stay for the show last night—somehow I was not in the mood," he added, a look of amusement on his face. "And then imagine my surprise when I saw you on the stage tonight."

"Yeah, imagine," Sam said drily, attempting to walk by him.

Jean-Claude took a step and stopped her. "I want to say only this," he told her in a low voice. "You were quite wonderful in this show. You are a talented dancer, an artist."

"Gee, thanks," Sam said sarcastically, trying to move around him once more.

"I underestimated you, Samantha," Jean-Claude said softly. "For this I apologize."

Sam stopped in her tracks and turned back to the Frenchman. "Did you say you *apologize*?" she asked incredulously.

"I did." He nodded solemnly. "But I did not know then that you were an artist," he added.

Sam put her hands on her hips and stared at him. "Oh, so you think that makes it okay? Well, I've got news for you, Jean-Claude. Treating a woman like an object is never okay. Just because you're filthy rich," she continued, "you don't think you have to see us mere mortals as real people. Well, think again, babe. And your apology is *not* accepted!"

Sam swept past Jean-Claude, with Emma and Carrie behind her. On her way by, for just a moment, Sam looked into Marie's eyes. They were full of tears.

"Sam, you are unbelievable!" Emma exclaimed when they reached the main hallway.

"I'm so proud of you," Carrie added. "God, I wish I had that moment on videotape."

"Girlfriends, I have to tell you," Sam said with an enormous grin, "that was one of the most satisfying moments of my life."

At that moment, Sam felt invincible. *I really can do anything I set my mind to*, she realized. *I can be a professional dancer, if I'm willing to work at it. And one day, when I'm ready, I can even face all those strangers in California.*

"Hey, you know what I really, really want to do right now?" Sam asked her friends impulsively.

"What?" Emma and Carrie asked at the same time.

"I want to go visit Pres, the mammal who has loved me through it all!" she said dramatically.

"I thought you told me his real name was Wilson," Emma said as they ran down the hall toward the dolphin tank.

"He'll always be Pres to me," Sam said.

As soon as Pres noticed Sam he swam to the glass and bumped it gently.

"Come on!" Sam called and hurried out the side door that led to the outdoor portion of the dolphin tank.

"Here, Pres!" Sam called.

And sure enough, the dolphin with the striking markings flew into the air, giving a cry of happiness.

"Now, that's love," Carrie said, laughing at the dolphin's antics.

And as the three girls stood there, each thought about her own life. Carrie thought about how different loving Billy was from a fling with Matt. Emma thought about how really getting to know her father might open up a whole new loving relationship. And Sam . . . Sam thought about how much she loved her real family—the one that had raised her—and the possibility of learning to love that other family in California.

"Maybe it really is possible," Sam whispered.

The only answer was the happy sound of the dolphin's loving chatter.

To Sam, it definitely sounded like a yes.

ONE

This is a day I'll remember my whole life, Darcy Laken thought as she looked down at the diploma the principal, Dr. Green, had just handed her. It was a perfect June afternoon, and her mother, father, three brothers, and two sisters were all sitting out there on the lawn watching her high school graduation. And the most exciting part was still to come.

"The Belinda Kramer Award for Athletic Excellence is an important tradition here at Kennedy High," the principal was saying from the podium.

This was it, the moment Darcy had been waiting for. Her heart beat double time in her chest. *Please let me win,* she prayed silently, her white-knuckled fingers clenched tightly around her diploma. *I've got to win.*

"As you know," Dr. Green continued, "Belinda Kramer was a student here at

Kennedy High from 1971 until she graduated in 1975. And as you also know, Belinda made our school, our town, and our country proud when she won not one but two gold medals for swimming in the 1976 summer Olympics in Montreal, Canada. Tragically, Belinda died two short years later from bone cancer."

A sad murmur went through the crowd. Everyone in Bangor knew this story as well as if Belinda Kramer had been a member of their own family. Darcy realized it was the stories she'd heard about Belinda that had made her want to become a diver in the first place.

"Belinda's family began a wonderful scholarship fund in her name, with the scholarship to be given every year to the best female athlete in the senior class here at Kennedy High," the principal continued. "But not only must the winner be the best athlete. She must also be a person of character and moral fiber, a young woman who upholds the very spirit of the Olympic games."

"It's you, I know it's you!" Suki Lamb, Darcy's best friend, whispered excitedly in Darcy's ear. She grabbed Darcy's arm and squeezed it.

Darcy was too nervous even to answer

Suki. The scholarship would mean so much to her. Even with the diving scholarship she'd been offered at the University of Maine, she still needed money for books, for food, for just plain living. No way could her parents afford to help her, much as they'd like to.

As Darcy closed her eyes even more tightly, willing the principal to call her name, all the years she'd spent perfecting her diving came rushing back to her, like a movie on fast-forward. The sacrifices her family had made, the hours upon hours at the pool diving again and again and again . . .

"And so it is with great pride," the principal's sonorous voice boomed, "that I announce the winner of the Belinda Kramer Award for Athletic Excellence, a scholarship in the amount of ten thousand dollars . . ."

Please let it be me. Please . . .

"Marianne Elizabeth Reed!"

Everyone applauded. Marianne and her friends squealed and hugged one another, then Marianne ran up to the podium.

But for Darcy Laken, time stopped.

Marianne Reed, the perky blond head cheerleader and baton twirler, the daughter of the city council president, had won instead of her.

"You got ripped, Laken," Kenny Monroe snorted from the row behind Darcy. "Athletic excellence in baton twirling? Gimme a break!"

"God, Darcy, I'm so sorry," Suki said softly. "I just can't believe this happened."

"It's no biggie," Darcy said, clamping her jaw shut hard to prevent herself from crying. She felt as if everyone in the senior class was looking at her to see how she was taking it. Well, no way was she going to give them the satisfaction of seeing her cry. The last time she'd cried in front of those other students, she'd been fourteen years old, and she'd vowed then that she'd never, ever let it happen again . . .

"No way am I wearing this, Mom," fourteen-year-old Darcy stated, looking down at herself in the terrible shiny brown dress with the excruciating cap sleeves.

It was the day before the first day of school. Darcy would be beginning the ninth grade—in high school at long last. Not only that, but Darcy's intelligence and excellent grades had gotten her into the magnet school in Bangor for smart kids, Kennedy High. The brightest—and often wealthiest—kids in the city all went to Kennedy. Darcy was so excited about it, she could hardly sleep at night. No more going to a school where kids actually brought weapons to school, where you took your life in your hands just trying to get from class to class. Everything would be different now.

Darcy was determined to be a great student, to look good, to fit in. She knew the first impression she made would be crucial. Just the night before she'd studied herself in the full-length mirror in the bathroom, trying to see what her new fellow classmates would see. Her long black hair was shiny and luxurious. Her violet eyes were thickly lashed—a little mascara would make them look even bigger. So far so good.

Then her eyes scanned her image from neck to feet, and she sighed deeply. How had she gotten so tall and so big so fast? She'd shot up two inches over the summer, and she'd already been the tallest girl in her class. Now she stood five feet nine inches in her stocking feet. And then there was her body. There was no way around it—she was big. Not fat—she could see she wasn't really fat. But just like her dad and her brothers, she had a big-boned, athletic body, and there was nothing she could do to change that.

Now that she'd grown so much, none of

her school clothes from the year before fit anymore. Even if Kennedy High allowed kids to wear jeans—which it didn't—hers were now two inches too short. So her mother had gone out shopping for school clothes, and this thing *was what she had brought home.*

"It's a nice dress, honey," her mother said, brushing a piece of lint off the full skirt that came down to Darcy's shins.

"It's horrible and you know it," Darcy seethed. "I hate it. No one in high school dresses like this."

"Well, maybe I could jazz it up a little," her mother suggested, deep lines appearing between her brows. "Some fancy buttons, maybe."

"Fancy buttons?" Darcy screeched. How could her mother be so totally, completely out of it? "Look, forget it," she said, pulling the loathsome garment over her head. "We'll take it back and I'll go shopping with you for something decent." Darcy threw the dress on the couch. "You should have just let me go with you in the first place. Where did you get it, anyway?"

Her mother began to fiddle with the buttons on the front of her faded sweater—something she did whenever she was anxious. "I think we can fix up this dress, Darcy, really."

Darcy zipped up her too-short jeans and stared at her mother. "We can't, Mom. Honest."

"Well, honey, I don't think we can return it," her mother said, fiddling even more anxiously with her buttons.

"Okay, so we'll exchange it," Darcy said. "Where'd you get it?"

"Well, um . . ." Darcy's mom began, her eyes not meeting Darcy's.

"It's okay if it's K Mart, Mom," Darcy said gently, buttoning her cotton blouse. Her mother knew Darcy hated it when she shopped at K Mart, but the clothes there were at least affordable.

"I got it at the Salvation Army," Darcy's mother said at last.

Darcy's fingers stopped on the last button of her shirt. "You what?"

This time her mother looked her right in the eye. "The Salvation Army," her mother repeated, holding her head high. "I didn't take you shopping with me because I didn't want you to feel embarrassed."

Darcy sat heavily on their worn sofa. "But . . ." she began.

"But nothing," her mother said firmly. She sat on the couch next to Darcy. "With

your dad out of work and all the medical bills, things are real tight right now."

"I know," Darcy said in a low voice. Her father had had a stroke just three months earlier, and was now home from the hospital but bedridden. Even in the best of times her dad's job as an auto mechanic and her mom's job as a waitress had barely made ends meet for a family of seven. Now with her dad out of work, possibly forever, they got public assistance to supplement her mom's income. It was something Darcy hated even to think about.

"Everyone needed new shoes, and Dean had to have that dental work done," her mother said. "Well, we just can't afford more than this right now, Darcy." She took her daughter's hand. "I'm sorry."

Darcy saw the pain etched in her mother's eyes. She'd aged so much since her husband's stroke! Darcy threw her arms around her mother and hugged her fiercely. "It's okay, Mom," she said. "The dress isn't really that bad. A lot of kids wear clothes from secondhand shops. It's actually kind of cool."

Her mother's answering smile loosened the terrible tightening in Darcy's throat. She couldn't stand to see her mother upset. "I'll add a belt and stuff," Darcy said, smiling brightly.

"You're sure?" her mother asked.

"Sure I'm sure," Darcy said.

That evening she fixed up the dress as best she could—she took off the cap sleeves and added a patent-leather belt that matched her patent-leather flats, which still fit if she jammed her feet into them.

The next morning she got on the school bus feeling hopeful. Perhaps her dress would even be considered trendy. But she knew it was going to be a nightmare after all when she saw the face of her best friend, Suki Lamb, as soon as she got on the bus.

Suki had gotten into Kennedy, too. Although her family was poor also, they weren't as poor as the Lakens. Suki had on a new miniskirt and a flowered T-shirt that looked just darling.

"What are you wearing?" Suki asked in horror as Darcy took a seat next to her.

"It's hip," Darcy said, swinging her hair over one shoulder. Suki didn't say anything else. Darcy sensed she didn't want to hurt her feelings.

The bus headed toward the wealthier neighborhoods, closer to the high school. Now other kids got on the bus, dressed in cool outfits that Darcy had seen in the display windows at the mall. They all seemed to know each other and they laughed and screamed at each other, standing in the aisles to talk, giving the bus driver the finger when he told them to sit down. It seemed to Darcy that some of the kids were looking at her and pointing and whispering, but she ignored them and talked with Suki all the way to school.

Just as Darcy was getting off the school bus she heard a girl with blond curls whisper to another girl, "I'm not kidding! I saw that rag at the Salvation Army when I went in with my mother to make a donation." Both girls turned to look at Darcy. She held her head high and walked right by them.

Darcy found out quickly who the blond-haired girl was—Marianne Reed, Miss Everything. And by noon, Marianne had told everyone just where Darcy had purchased her dress. Everyone was laughing, whispering, tittering behind Darcy's back. At lunchtime she took her sandwich outside to sit by herself in the sun. Suki was the only person she knew, but Suki had a different lunch period. Darcy closed her eyes and lifted her face to the sun, wishing she were anyplace else except in Bangor, Maine, at Kennedy High School wearing a brown dress from the Salvation Army.

"There she is," Darcy heard someone whisper. "Can you believe that dress?"

"She looks like the Jolly Brown Giant," another voice guffawed, and both of the girls cracked up.

"Well, what can you expect?" the first voice said. "She's just plain white trash."

Darcy opened her eyes. It was Marianne Reed, and she had just called Darcy white trash. Darcy had been raised to believe that a Laken always stood up for herself and her family. She'd also been taught to box by her older brother Sean.

Darcy stood up, wiped the crumbs off her fingers, and walked calmly over to Marianne.

Then she pulled back her fist and decked her.

It turned out that Darcy had broken Marianne's nose. She got called to Dr. Green's office and suspended on her very first day of school. Her mother was at work at the restaurant, so the principal talked to her father and told him that Darcy had been suspended. Sean came to pick Darcy up in the family's beat-up old Ford.

By the time Darcy left the principal's office, it seemed as if everyone at Kennedy High knew what had happened. As Darcy walked down the hall to meet Sean, every-

one was laughing and jeering at her. And she couldn't help herself—she began to cry. Sobs overtook her before she could make it out to the car. It was like feeding hungry sharks—her tears made the kids taunt her even more. Now they knew she was weak. Now they knew they could get to her.

And that was the first impression Darcy Frances Laken had made on her first day of high school.

That was then, this is now, Darcy reminded herself, giving herself a mental shake. She breathed deeply and willed back the tears that were threatening to overflow from her eyes. After all, she'd gone on to make some great friends at Kennedy. She'd been on the honor roll, been in two school plays, and excelled in the athletic department. And somewhere around her sophomore year, she'd grown into her looks and become comfortable with being tall and strapping. Some of the cutest guys in the school had started asking her out, and she'd dated fairly often. But still, somehow having Marianne, who didn't need the money at all, beat her out for the athletic scholarship—Marianne, who had remained her nemesis for all four years of high school—brought the old pain back as if it had happened yesterday.

The ceremony finally ended, and the seniors went running to their families for hugs and congratulations. Darcy made her way through the crowd to her own family and hugged her mother, then her father.

"I'm proud of you, girl," her dad said with his slight Irish brogue. Darcy's father, Connor, had come to the United States from Ireland with his family when he was six years old.

"Thanks, Daddy," Darcy said, grinning at him. She worried about him; she just couldn't help it. Ever since the stroke four years earlier he'd grown increasingly frail. And for a man like Connor Laken, who had always prided himself on his strong body, it was a bitter pill to swallow.

"So you've gone and done it," Sean said, hugging his little sister. At twenty-four, Sean was the oldest. His bright blue eyes, red hair, and fair skin were in sharp contrast to his sister's looks. But then Sean, Dean, and Patsi had inherited their father's Irish coloring, and Darcy, Patrick, and the baby, Lilly, had inherited their mother's dark coloring.

"Pick me up!" Lilly cried, pulling on Darcy's white graduation robe. Darcy picked up her three-year-old sister and swung her in the air.

Lilly was such a sweetheart—everyone in the family doted on her. Darcy suspected that Lilly was an accident, that before her, their parents had considered themselves done with having children. After all, Patsi was the next youngest and she was already in eighth grade. But the fact that her mother had conceived a baby after her father's stroke seemed to make Connor so happy—and now Lilly was the joy of the entire family.

"When are you going to graduate and earn your keep, huh, little one?" Connor asked the giggling Lilly.

"I didn't even start school yet!" Lilly protested, snuggling her face into Darcy's hair.

"Well, let's get it over and done with. Time's a-wasting!" her father chided playfully.

"Don't you listen to him, Lilly," Darcy told her sister fiercely. "One day you're going to go to college, and you're going to be someone very, very special!"

A lump formed in Darcy's throat all over again. If she could only manage to go to college in the fall, she would be the first one in the family to go beyond high school. But how was she ever going to afford it now?

"We'll figure something out," Shanna

Laken said to her daughter softly, as if she had read Darcy's mind.

"You should have won the damned scholarship," twenty-year-old Dean said. "It wasn't fair."

"Don't curse, son," Connor said automatically.

Dean rolled his eyes. He worked in a shipyard, and heard things every day that would make your hair stand on end.

"Hey, Darcy!" Suki called, running over to her. "Come with me. I want my mom to get a picture of us together."

"Let me get one of you two before you run off," Shanna Laken said, lifting the family's inexpensive camera. Darcy put her arm around the diminutive Suki, who barely came to her shoulder, and they both smiled for the camera.

"Get one of all of us!" thirteen-year-old Patsi suggested, and the whole family crowded in as Suki took their picture.

"I'll be right back," Darcy promised her family. She knew her mother had been scrimping and saving to take the whole family out to Riches—an inexpensive family-style restaurant—in honor of her graduation.

"Oh, please, look what crawled out from under its rock," Suki muttered when she and Darcy walked over to where her mother and brother were waiting. There was Marianne chatting with Suki's older brother, Andy. Andy had just finished his freshman year at the University of Maine, and Andy was, as Suki said, "a hunka-hunka-burnin' love"—or so all her friends told her. But then Suki said that about Darcy's older brothers too.

"I think it's incredible that you've already been published in *The Poison Pen*!" Marianne was gushing to Andy. *The Poison Pen* was the literary magazine at the University of Maine, and Andy had recently had one of his short stories printed there.

"God, she's disgusting," Suki whispered to Darcy. "She couldn't get him to ask her out last year when he was still at Kennedy, and he's not about to change his mind now that he's in college."

"Oh, hi, Suki, hi, Darcy," Marianne said perkily when Suki and Darcy walked over.

"Hi," Darcy said flatly, wishing that Marianne would simply go away.

"Too bad about the scholarship," Marianne told Darcy, shaking her curls away from her face. "I know you need that money *infinitely* more than I do."

"I'll get by," Darcy said coolly, staring Marianne in the eye.

"Good," Marianne said with a smile. "You

know, confidentially, you're probably a better athlete than me."

"Garfield is a better athlete than you," Suki snapped.

"But the scholarship is about more than that," Marianne continued, ignoring Suki. "It has to do with character."

Darcy could feel the heat coming to her face. "Is that so?"

"It is," Marianne said earnestly. "And, well, no offense, Darcy, but the winner is supposed to represent Kennedy High. And you are not exactly what I would call representative of our community."

Darcy felt her fingers curl into a tight fist. She was itching, dying to pull back and punch that smug smile off Marianne's face. *You're not fourteen anymore and you can control your temper*, Darcy told herself, willing herself to unclench her fist. "You're entitled to your opinion," she managed to get out in a steely voice.

"No you're not," tiny Suki spat out, staring at Marianne. "Your opinions are as stupid and narrow-minded as you are."

Marianne grinned even more broadly, and Suki took a step toward her, but Darcy stopped her by putting a restraining hand on Suki's arm. "Forget it," she murmured.

"Temper, temper," Marianne chided. She

laughed a tinkly laugh. "Well, I've got to run. Bye-bye now. Bye, Andy." She turned on her heel to head back to her large circle of friends and family.

And then the strangest thing happened.

It was as if a special light went on in Darcy's brain, as if her mind were an X-ray machine seeing things that no one else could see. For just a split second, instead of seeing Marianne, Darcy saw *into* Marianne, and then she saw Marianne's future.

She saw a tumor growing in Marianne's skull.

"Are you okay?" Suki asked Darcy.

"Wh-what?" Darcy asked. The flash was gone.

"You looked really weird there for a moment," Suki said.

"I'm fine," Darcy said.

But that wasn't true. Every once in a while, something similar happened. Sometimes things came to her in a dream, sometimes in this bizarre flash of light. But sometimes, somehow, Darcy just knew things.

When she was ten years old she'd had a flash in which she saw fire, just hours before their clothes dryer blew up in the basement, setting the lower part of their house ablaze. Another time she'd had a dream that her father was talking to her as if he were a baby. This had happened just two nights before his stroke, which had temporarily reduced his speech to garbled baby talk. Darcy had no control over the flashes, didn't know what they were or why she had them. The whole thing scared her so much that she usually tried to push it to the back of her mind.

But once again, Darcy just knew something. Marianne Elizabeth Reed had a deadly tumor growing in her brain, and Darcy Laken was the only one who knew it.

SUNSET ISLAND MAILBOX

Dear Cherie,

I love the Sunset Island *series. I can't imagine not being able to read your novels. You are the best author I've ever read because your books are so real. My question is: Does Sunset Island really exist?*

Your biggest fan,
Jody Daigle
Jacquet River, Canada

Dear Jody,

This is a question I get asked a lot. I'm sorry to say that Sunset Island doesn't really exist—I wish it did! I'd love to hear from any of you who live on or have visited a resort island like Sunset Island. Who knows—your experiences might even be included in a future book!

Best,
Cherie

Dear Cherie,

I recently read your Sunset Reunion *and have read all the other books in the series. My favorite part was when Carrie and Emma arrived at the hotel in Disney World. Do you enjoy being an author? How did you become an author? Who are the girls on the covers of your books? Can you send me an autographed picture or information about yourself?*

Sincerely,
Gina Savino
Brooklyn, New York

Dear Gina,

Yes, I love being an author. For every budding writer out there, remember—there will always be people who say you can't succeed, but the only real failure is not trying at all. And in order to learn to write, you must read, read, read! As for the girls on the covers, they are New York City actresses and models who were picked from hundreds considered for the job. Do they look like Carrie, Sam, and Emma to you? I will be sending you a picture—thanks for asking! Hey, how about sending me one of you, too?

Best,
Cherie

Dear Cherie,

I've never read anything as great as the Sunset Island *series. When I read I feel like I'm right there with Emma, Carrie, and Sam. Did you base Jeff Hewitt on your husband? Are any of these characters based on certain people? You did a great job on Lorell and Diana! Keep up the good work!*

Your #1 fan,
Linda Hanan
Skokie, Illinois

Dear Linda,

Good guess—I did base Jeff Hewitt on my husband, Jeff! Lorell and Diana (aren't they despicable?) are somewhat based on a girl named Diane who I knew in junior high. She seemed to live to make my life miserable. Now I realize she was probably extremely insecure and unhappy--which is why she was so nasty. But at the time it just hurt! Have any of you had an experience like this? Write and tell me about it—maybe I can use it in the continuing adventures of Lorell and Diana!

Best,
Cherie

Dear Readers,
Wow, do you guys ever write some great letters! I must be the luckiest author in the world to have readers like you. It means so much to me that you care enough to take the time to write and share your lives with me. Also, many of you have had some terrific ideas for the series—story lines you'd like to see, characters you like and dislike, etc. It's so helpful to me. I guarantee that some of these ideas are going to make it into future books.

I love hearing from all of you, so please keep those letters coming. I think they are so great I want to share them with the world! If it's okay to print your letter, please say so. And as always, I promise to answer each and every letter personally. You deserve it.

See you on the island!

Cherie

Cherie Bennett
c/o General Licensing Company
24 West 25th Street
New York, New York 10010

SEND IN THIS COUPON AND BE ONE OF THE FIRST TO READ

SUNSET AFTER DARK

GET PSYCHED FOR AN ALL-NEW ADVENTURE IN MARCH '93 FROM

CHERIE BENNETT

Darcy Laken is a beautiful, street-smart eighteen-year-old befriended by Emma, Carrie, and Sam in *Sunset Scandal*. She lives on the *other* side of Sunset Island—in an old and foreboding house on a hill where she works for the eccentric Mason family. When Darcy and Molly Mason find themselves in danger, Darcy gets a premonition about who is responsible. But when she asks for help from the cute guy who is threatening to steal her heart, he doesn't believe her!

Don't miss a single adventure featuring Darcy!
SUNSET AFTER MIDNIGHT coming in April
SUNSET AFTER HOURS coming in May

FREE!

Fill out this coupon! If yours is ONE OF THE FIRST 1,000 COUPONS RECEIVED, we'll send you a FREE copy of *Sunset After Dark*, the first in the all *new Sunset Island* adventures.

Print legibly for mailing purposes

Send to: SUNSET PROMOTION
Fulfillment Services
P.O. BOX 253
Nanticoke, PA 18634

Name ______________________________

Street ______________________________

City ________________ State _____ Zip _______

Offer expires 12/30/92. Void where prohibited. Allow 8-10 weeks to receive your book.
Offer limited to residents of the U.S.